NOT EXACTLY
MINNESOTA

The student parking lot was filled with Porsches, BMWs, Mercedes', and Corvettes.

Brandon glanced over at his sister and said, "It looks like an auto show."

"I think we're going to need a raise in our allowances." Brenda looked around in disbelief.

"Not just a raise," said Brandon. "We're going to need three or four allowances apiece."

"Just for transportation," Brenda said as she nodded.

After Brandon finally found a parking place, he and Brenda just sat in Mondale looking around, stunned. "This is even worse than I imagined it would be," Brenda whispered. "Every one of these kids looks as if they just stepped out of a music video . . . ."

Coming soon from HarperPaperbacks

Beverly Hills, 90210–Exposed!

Beverly Hills, 90210–No Secrets

SPELLING ENT. INC.

A
Novel by
MEL GILDEN

HarperPaperbacks
A Division of HarperCollins*Publishers*

HarperPaperbacks   *A Division of* HarperCollins*Publishers*
10 East 53rd Street, New York, N.Y. 10022

Copyright © 1991 by Torand, a Spelling Entertainment Company

Cover photo courtesy of Fox Broadcasting Co.
Back cover photo courtesy of E.J.Camp

First printing: November 1991

Printed in the United States of America

HarperPaperbacks and colophon are trademarks of HarperCollins*Publishers*

10 9 8 7 6 5 4 3

**BASED ON THE TELEVISION SERIES CREATED
BY DARREN STAR**

The stories in this book are based on teleplays by

Darren Star, Charles Rosin, David Stenn and Amy Spies

Contents

1

Fun in the sun
and education, too

IT WAS THE FIRST DAY OF THE FALL SEMESTER,
and the West Beverly High parking lot was a zoo. As
far as Brandon Walsh could tell, it was a very radical,
bitchen, and superior kind of zoo, but it was a zoo
nonetheless. He'd never before seen so many Jags,
Mercedes', BMWs, Porsches, or 'vettes in one place in
his life, each one gleaming in the early-morning
California sun.

He was painfully aware of the car he was driving, a
1983 Honda Accord. The Walsh family called it
Mondale, after the former senator from Minnesota. It
was kind of a joke.

In Minnesota, Mondale had seemed like a great
car. But here in the student parking lot, Brandon felt as
if he were driving an old broken-down vegetable truck
or even a *teacher's* car! The only things his car had in

common with all the others in the student lot were four wheels, a gasoline engine, and a need for a place to park.

Brandon glanced over at his sister and said, "It looks like an auto show."

Brenda looked around in disbelief. "I think we're going to need a raise in our allowances."

Brenda was a very cute girl with long, dark hair and high cheekbones. Brandon himself was on the cute list of many high-school girls back in Minnesota. But if anyone had mentioned it to him, he would have shrugged, shaken his head, and denied it with some embarrassment.

"Not just a raise," said Brandon. "We're going to need three or four allowances apiece."

Brenda nodded. "Just for transportation," she said.

After Brandon found a parking place, at last, he and Brenda just sat in Mondale looking around, stunned. "This is even worse than I imagined it would be," Brenda said. "Every one of these kids looks as if they just stepped out of a music video."

It was true. Brandon saw no ties, no charcoal gray pants, no sport coats. These kids were not formal, but they were all very hip. They were wearing what the kids in Minnesota would be wearing next year. In two years, maybe. Still, there was no point upsetting Brenda even more. He said, "You're not exactly a bag lady, Brenda."

"Who knows what the bag ladies around here look like?"

"Yeah. They probably wear diamond tiaras."

Brenda looked at her brother. Brandon laughed and she shook her head and joined him. They got out of the car before anybody could associate them with it and walked toward the main gate. "Mighty hot for September," Brandon said.

"Mighty hot for September in Minnesota," Brenda said. A guy in a Hawaiian shirt and white shorts nearly ran them down with his skateboard.

As she sized up the student body Brenda said, "Look for me at lunch."

"Sure." Brandon himself was a little preoccupied. Everything the girls in Beverly Hills wore was shorter or tighter or more colorful than what the girls wore in Minnesota. They all looked like movie stars. This was Beverly Hills. Maybe they *were* all movie stars.

Brenda looked at Brandon with some intensity and went on, "I don't want to look like some geek who doesn't have any friends."

"Great. Sitting together, we'll look like *a pair* of geeks who don't have any friends."

"*Bran*don," she said warningly.

Brandon put up his hands in surrender. "Joke. Okay?"

The day was already interesting, if nothing else. Brandon tried to just relax and enjoy it. On his way into the main building, he picked up a copy of the school newspaper, the *Beverly Blaze*, and nodded as he studied it critically.

Brenda walked quickly down the hall. She had an armload of books. Clenched in her teeth was a small sheet of yellow paper that told her where to go. Or rather, it told her the numbers of the rooms she was supposed to be in at particular hours. She didn't exactly know where they were. Each of the buildings had its own numbering system. The school was humongous.

She'd gotten lost more times than she could count and she feared that she was lost again. She shifted some books and studied the yellow sheet. She'd remembered the room number correctly, but it didn't seem to be anywhere around here. Imagine going through all this trouble just to find chemistry class!

Kids ducked into classrooms like rabbits down rabbit holes. Soon she was alone but for a spectacularly enormous girl with overteased hair. The leather outfit she wore was too tight and bulged in all the wrong places; an entire notions counter of metal bracelets jingled on her arms, and for her own reasons she showed off legs that would have looked better on a piano.

The leather queen may have been a perfectly nice girl, but even if she was not, Brenda was encouraged by her appearance. Brenda would be only the second dorkiest dresser at West Beverly High.

The leather queen swung a door open wide and went into the room beyond. Good grief, that was her chemistry room! The leather queen was a classmate! Brenda took a couple of deep breaths. Her parents had always reminded her not to judge people by their appearance. Easy for them to say. They didn't go to high school in Beverly Hills.

To save herself from having to rearrange her books again so she could open the door, Brenda hurled herself into the room just as the door was closing.

The bell rang as Brenda stepped up next to the leather queen, the object of curiosity of the class and of a thin balding guy in a lab coat. He had to be the teacher. Mr. Ridley, if Brenda remembered correctly. He sneered at her delicately and studied her over the top of his wire-rim glasses.

She and the leather queen had evidently caught him

in the middle of a thought. He ignored them and said, "Choose your seat carefully. The person sitting next to you will be your lab partner for the rest of the semester."

Each table had a silver faucet on it. Maybe it dispensed gas. It certainly was not a water faucet. More important, each table had room for two students, and almost every table had a full complement.

Now that she was here, Brenda wasn't sure what to do next. The leather queen had no such problem. She lumbered to an empty seat next to a pretty girl who had long blond hair and loomed over her like King Kong over Fay Wray. The blond girl smiled as if she were learning to enjoy a broken toe and said, "Sorry, this seat's taken."

"By who?" the leather queen rumbled. Could a high-school girl really have a voice like Darth Vader's?

To Brenda's surprise, the blond girl pointed to her and said, "That girl."

The leather queen turned her entire body to glare at Brenda with suspicion.

The blonde waved at Brenda as if attracting her attention in a crowd and called, "Hi! Over here!"

Brenda looked to see if anyone was behind her. There was not. The blonde was very cute, near awesome. Everything she wore screamed a designer's name. Was it possible this Bev Hills princess was talking to her?

The expression on the blonde's face was no more natural than the smile on a happy-face button. "I saved you a seat!" she cried.

As Brenda moved among the tables toward the blonde the leather queen lumbered on to find a different victim. Brenda carefully lowered her stack of books and gratefully sat down.

Like a con on the prison exercise yard, Brenda leaned closer to the blonde and said, "Thanks. But I think you're confusing me with somebody else."

The blonde whispered, "That's okay. I'm just being friendly."

Brenda's eyebrows went up. She'd heard strange things about people in California. Could this girl mean . . . ?

"I'm Kelly," the blonde said.

Brenda pushed her suspicions from her mind and decided to accept Kelly at face value, just as she was willing to reject the leather queen. Brenda said, "I'm Brenda."

"Hi," Kelly said, and smiled a genuine smile. The smile went away and she asked earnestly, "Are you smart?"

What did that mean? Maybe this girl wasn't perverted but just bizarre. Or maybe everybody in Beverly Hills asked total strangers this kind of question. Hedging a little, Brenda said, "Sort of." Maybe the smart kids had no friends. It turned out that way sometimes in Minnesota.

Kelly cocked her head in the direction of Mr. Ridley and said, "This class is a real bitch. I'll need all the help I can get." She smiled philosophically.

Brenda smiled back, understanding now where Kelly was coming from. It looked to Brenda as if she'd made her first friend at West Beverly High.

Meanwhile, in a classroom across campus, Brandon sat through his Spanish II class. He was shocked to discover it would be conducted entirely in Spanish, but felt a little less nervous when he noticed that his fellow students were as terrified as he was.

"Very bogus," the guy next to him said. "Miss Montes gets paid for speaking her mother tongue."

The guy was Steve Sanders, a tall dude with short curly blond hair, a perpetually world-weary expression, and a very heavy attitude. He'd have everyone believe he'd seen and done everything before, maybe twice. Brandon decided that in his jeans, white T-shirt, motorcycle jacket, and wraparound shades, Steve had overdone it a little in the *coolth* department. But the guy was amusing and interesting and he seemed to need a friend, so Brandon tried to be one.

Also in the class was the usual mix of nerds, dorks, dweebs, soshes, and kids who were, like himself, more or less normal. Despite the bogus nature of her job, Ms. Montes was a very foxy Hispanic woman whose taste in clothing ran to tight sweaters. Which was okay with Brandon, except that the sweaters—or rather, what filled them—sometimes made it difficult for Brandon to concentrate on the lesson.

One girl, one of the few who wore glasses, seemed to have no difficulty with the lessons for any reason. She spoke Spanish like a native, or at least well enough to please Ms. Montes. The girl was all business. She had not spent a lot of time putting on makeup or fixing her hair. She was pretty in a perky, nonspectacular way.

Nothing about her was hip, but it was all very functional—preppie rather than yuppie. She wore jeans, practical shoes, and a simple blouse. Her blue nylon backpack displayed no symbols of favorite vacation spots, preferred clothing manufacturers, or totally hot bands. If it hadn't been for her obvious facility with Spanish, and the feverish intensity of her desire to learn, she would have faded right into the woodwork.

She was cute. She was different. In a mild way, Brandon was fascinated.

Learning Spanish was a heady experience when you didn't have English to fall back on.

When class was over, Brandon pulled out his copy of the *Beverly Blaze,* now a little wrinkled, and found the information he wanted.

He thought he had West Beverly High geography down to a science, but he got lost twice on his way to the *Blaze* editorial office.

The office was a regular classroom, but with fewer desks and more equipment. The three kids laboring over computer terminals barely glanced up as he entered. At one end of the room, a honey-blond girl sat reading long sheets of galley proofs. With the hair hanging in front of her face that way, she could have been anybody.

Brandon waited for somebody to notice him. Nobody did. He coughed. Still no response. He once more checked the masthead of the paper for the managing editor's name, and said, "Is Andrea Zuckerman around?"

The girl with the proofs looked up and said, "Yeah. Right here." It was the girl from the Spanish class. The one who knew all the Spanish.

"*Hola,*" Brandon said with surprise.

She blinked at him without interest, one tough cookie.

Maybe she just doesn't recognize me, Brandon thought. He turned up the power on his smile a few watts and said, "We're in Spanish together. I'm Brandon Walsh."

"*Hola,*" Andrea said without enthusiasm. She glanced back at her galleys. If she'd been less of a lady, she'd have tapped her foot.

Out of desperation, Brandon took this as encouragement. He turned around a chair next to the desk and, as he sat down, said, "I want to write for the paper."

"Can you write?" Andrea asked as if she suspected he might be faking his knowledge of the alphabet.

One tough cookie, Brandon thought. He said, "I was the sports editor at my old school." He dropped his voice as if he were admitting he wore the wrong brand of running shoes and said, "In Minnesota."

Andrea nodded.

"You know," Brandon said. "Garrison Keillor?"

"We're a little provincial here in Beverly Hills, but I've heard of Minnesota. I'll give you a test story. You can cover either toxic-waste disposal in our chemistry classes or the girls' water-polo match against Beverly High. Which one do you want?"

"We don't have a girls' water-polo team back where I come from, so I'll go for the new experience. What time's the game?"

Andrea shook her head and sighed. She said, "You definitely failed my test."

Brandon was aware that the clicking of tiny keys had stopped. He didn't want to turn to look, but he was sure that the three at the terminals were watching them. Watching *him*. Maybe it was all a joke. Until he learned otherwise, being a good sport was probably wise. He mustered all his warmth and said, "I don't get it."

Andrea explained as if she'd explained before. She seemed a little angry when she said, "Whenever a guy wants to work for the paper, I ask him whether he wants to cover the toxic-waste story or girls' water-polo. Not one guy has *ever* chosen the toxic-waste story." She studied him and asked sarcastically, "Why do you think that is, Brandon?"

"Human nature?" Brandon asked. It would be the wrong answer. Whatever he said would be the wrong answer.

Andrea lined up her pencils and straightened her galleys while she said, "No offense, Brandon, but this is the top-ranked high-school paper in the country, and I intend to keep it that way. So put aside your dreams of editing the swimsuit issue of *Sports Illustrated* and consider long hours, firm deadlines, and total commitment. Still interested?"

Brandon shook his head and grinned. He said, "Wow! You are intense."

Andrea's mouth twitched as her composure leaked away. In a few seconds she was grinning back at Brandon. She shrugged and said, "I know. But that's what it takes to do what we do around here. So if you don't want to make the sacrifices, I totally understand."

Brandon stood up and rubbed his hands together as if he were about to chop wood, "I guess I should start by interviewing the janitor."

"Custodial engineer."

Brandon nodded and walked toward the door. The school was tough. The women were tough. If he was going to make it here, he'd have to become tough too. His hand was on the doorknob when Andrea called out to him. "And Brandon?"

Brandon turned and waited for another zinger.

"Nice meeting you."

It was like being hit with a pillow when you were expecting a fist. Brandon was a little disoriented. He said, "Uh, yeah. Nice meeting you, too," and got out as fast as he could.

■ ■ ■

The cafeteria was just a cafeteria, Brenda thought with some relief. Like the cafeterias at the schools in Minneapolis, this one had long Formica-topped tables and chairs that had once been in better condition. A doorway led to benches out in the sunlight, but a lot of kids stayed inside because of the smog. No smog in Minneapolis. Chalk one up for good ol' Minneapolis.

Some of the food was familiar. Brenda had taken a burger and fries, for instance. But you could also get an individual pizza with sun-dried tomatoes on it. Sun-dried tomatoes looked like tiny deflated red balloons. Brenda decided to try them only after she'd gotten used to everything else in Beverly Hills.

On her tray, Kelly had an alfalfa-sprout-and-tofu salad. She had to watch her figure, she said. Why shouldn't *she* watch it, Brenda thought? All the guys did.

Kelly led Brenda away from the cash registers and they stood together looking for a good place to sit. One could not sit just anywhere. Kelly said, "You're going to need a native guide, Brenda. It's a good thing you met me when you did, before you made a false move that would brand you for life. West Beverly isn't like other schools. Kids here are richer. Some of their parents are celebs. Socially, it's really intense. I mean, if people saw you eating lunch with the wrong people, or worse yet, alone like that guy—" She used her chin to motion at some poor dweeb sitting by himself at one side of the room.

Brenda realized with some horror that Kelly's sample geek was Brandon and she began to guide Kelly in the other direction in what she hoped was a subtle way. She managed to maneuver them so that when they settled, Kelly's back was to Brandon. While they organized their plates and aluminum silverware, Brenda said, "I had great friends at my old school."

"In Minneapolis?"

"Well, yeah. Where else?"

Kelly went on as if Brenda had not spoken defensively. Inside, Brenda promised herself to lighten up. Kelly said, "But it's so cold. I could never deal with cold."

"You'd get over it."

"I'd get fat."

Brenda looked out through the walls, over mountain ranges, back to Minneapolis. "Yeah," she said dreamily. "It's great. All winter long you can eat whatever you want and hide the porkage under bulky sweaters. Christmas is always a total disaster, fat-wise."

Kelly laughed and said, "That's definitely not Beverly Hills. Somebody is always throwing a pool party. You never get a chance to really pig out." She lifted a shred of alfalfa sprout and looked at it. She shook it in Brenda's face and said, "Eat sprouts. Stay thin. Kelly would not steer you wrong."

As she listened to Kelly, Brenda became more and more aware that she had a lot to learn if she was going to be a social success at West Beverly High. For one thing, she would not eat another french fry as long as she lived. Brandon seemed to make friends without effort, but she didn't have that talent. She'd have to work at it. Still, Kelly was astonishingly beautiful, and she knew everything (except chemistry), and she was social to the max. And here she was, actually sitting with Brenda. Brenda shook her head with amazement.

"What's going on?" Kelly said. She'd been fixing her lipstick, and she was looking at something reflected in her mirror.

Brenda looked over Kelly's shoulder and saw that all the kids who were outside were staring and pointing at the sky. More kids poured out the door every second. Brenda and Kelly bussed their dishes and ran out the door in time to see words appearing in the sky, one letter at a time.

"How do they do that?" Brenda asked.

"Skytyping," Kelly said. "Five airplanes fly in formation and let out puffs of smoke that form letters. No skytyping in Minnesota?"

"We barely have airplanes," Brenda said.

"Yeah yeah. Sure sure. You came here in a covered wagon."

The message said: BACK TO SCHOOL JAM. FRIDAY NIGHT. 29150 SKYLINE DRIVE. BE THERE OR BE SQUARE.

Kelly said, "Oh, my God. That's Marianne Moore's house. She's incredibly rich, and a complete party girl. Her house is so big, you need a map to get around."

"This is amazing," Brenda said. "A skywritten—er, typed, party invitation? Is she really inviting the entire school? There must be eighteen hundred people—" She stopped when she saw the next bit of the message. It said NO FRESHMEN.

"Make that thirteen hundred," said Kelly. She grabbed Brenda's arm. "Let's go together."

Yes! Brenda thought triumphantly. With Kelly as her guide, everything would be awesome. "Sure," she said,

As she scanned the crowd outside, she saw

Brandon standing nearby. He caught her eye and waved. While Kelly watched the sky for further instructions, Brenda felt confident enough to wink back. Her brother nodded and gave her the thumbs-up.

2

Party down, dudes!

AS IT MUST TO ALL WEEKS, FRIDAY NIGHT
came at last. Marianne Moore's party was that evening,
but Brandon didn't feel he should go. He had a lot of
homework to do. He sprawled on his bed trying to concentrate on *A Tale of Two Cities*.

Besides, Brandon was not the major sosh that
Brenda made him out to be. Since the first day of classes, Brenda had made dozens of friends. Brandon had
met a lot of people, had had a few laughs, but not even
Steve Sanders had yet become a friend. Pitiful. That's
what it was. Just pitiful.

"You got it right, Dickens, old boy," Brandon said
out loud. "'It was the best of times. It was the worst of
times.'" The definition of a Beverly Hills party night
without a date.

Somebody knocked at the door, Brandon called

out, "Come in," and his dad entered. Mr. Walsh was a stocky, dark-haired man who was thinning a little on top. It was his promotion that had torn them up by their Minneapolis roots and planted them in Beverly Hills. He was generally a laid-back kind of guy with an interest in basketball, and now he lounged in Brandon's doorway wearing colorful sweats and his socks without shoes.

"Not going to the party? Your sister's been girding herself for hours," Mr. Walsh said nonchalantly.

"Lots of homework," Brandon said, and ran the flat of his hand over the book page. This was bizarre. The homework had to be done, of course, but not necessarily *tonight*. Brandon tried to ignore the fact that he didn't want to go to the party alone.

"After only a week?" Mr. Walsh said.

Brandon rolled over and sat on the edge of his bed. "This is West Beverly High, Dad. We have the biggest, the fastest, the best. As I am continually reminded."

Mr. Walsh stopped holding up the wall. "I hear that goes for the West Beverly High parties, too. Even for the new kids."

Mr. Walsh closed the door softly, leaving Brandon alone with Dickens. Here was his dad trying to convince him to go to a party. Dad was a great guy, but he just didn't understand. A horn honked in the street below. Brandon got up and went to look out the window.

The evening was cool, but not as cool as a September evening in Minneapolis would be. The sweet smell of night-blooming flowers washed in.

A BMW convertible was parked in the Walsh driveway. It could have been any color at all. In the weird arc streetlights, it was a putrid orange. More importantly, it contained four girls—Cathy, Donna, Michelle, and the unmistakable Kelly. Even from this distance and in this light, Brandon could see they had on sufficient war paint and the right kind of clothes to suggest that they planned to party hearty.

Brenda and Mrs. Walsh walked out to the car. Mrs. Walsh was a thin handsome woman who kept her hair in a practical but flattering flip. Brenda's movements were jerky and self-conscious. She was probably embarrassed about being seen with her mother, Brandon thought.

Brenda introduced her friends. And then Mrs. Walsh dropped her bomb. "So, when's your curfew?" she asked Kelly.

"Excuse me?" Kelly asked in disbelief.

"You see?" Brenda said as if Kelly's question had proved a point. Brandon noticed how Brenda cleverly got into the car before everything was decided. Kelly turned on the engine, and from where he was, Brandon could barely hear it hum.

"Midnight, okay?" Mrs. Walsh said.

"Ouch," grumbled Donna.

Kelly had the car moving now. It was not moving fast, but the motion lent a certain urgency to the discussion.

"Twelve-thirty!" Brenda called as the car reached the end of the driveway.

"Twelve-fifteen," Mrs. Walsh called after the car as it turned onto the street. She shook her head as the car moved away from her at increasing speed.

The entire scene below had been very entertaining, and Brandon wondered if, perhaps, he'd made a mistake opting for homework instead of what was certain to be a totally awesome party. For one thing, he now had proof that his sister would not be the only girl there. And not even in Beverly Hills was there a law against going to a party stag.

Brandon explained to his parents that he'd changed his mind about the party—which seemed to please them—and took Mondale. He drove above Sunset, along twisty streets lined with high-priced real estate behind even higher walls. The occasional streetlight cast spooky shadows from the branches of tall trees that more often than not hid street signs. The entire production said in a loud firm voice that if you didn't know your way around, you did not belong here.

Brandon finally found what had to be the party house and parked a few blocks away, hoping that nobody would notice what he'd arrived in. Actually, parking a few blocks away was no problem. Any closer to the house and the curbs were bumper to bumper.

The party site itself was less a house than it was a mansion on a grassy knoll. Brandon had seen buildings like it in *Citizen Kane* and *Gone With the Wind*. Just walking up the driveway to it from the street could win you a merit badge for hiking.

He would have knocked, but the front door was blocked open by a group of kids sitting against it. Beyond was a mad collage of dancing, talking, eating, and drinking, all done to a wild rock-and-roll beat. The clothes the kids wore in school seemed like religious-school uniforms compared to what they were wearing at this party. Extremes of color and fashion were everywhere, even on the guys. The girls ranged from cute to fine to totally awesome. Back in the house, glass shattered. Brandon wondered who this Marianne Moore was, anyhow. Did she have parents or what?

Brandon pushed himself in among the writhing

bodies, briefly found himself dancing with a pert brunette, and squeaked out wide French doors into the backyard, a place not much smaller than a country.

A couple of girls in bathing suits—candidates for that mythical swimsuit issue Andrea had warned him he'd never get a chance to edit—ran down to an indoor pool that looked over a pair of tennis courts. The courts had been converted into a dance floor by taking down the nets and putting up Japanese lanterns. Below the tennis courts, Los Angeles looked like a spilled jewel box. Music from what turned out to be a live band blasted his eardrums, even from this distance. What did the neighbors think? Did a place like this have neighbors? It seemed to be big enough to be a neighborhood unto itself.

Someone next to him said, "Hey, Brandon."

It was Steve Sanders from Spanish. Good, a friendly face. "Hey, Steve."

Steve took a pull from a brown paper bag he carried and sighed with something more than pleasure. He said, "So, my man, what's your type?"

"Type?" asked Brandon.

"Blond? Brunette? Short? Tall? Good legs? Good buns?" He suggestively finished, "Or what?" and leered before he took another hit from his bag.

"Yes," said Brandon enthusiastically.

"You have come to the right place," Steve said. He put an arm around Brandon's shoulder and guided him into the heart of the party.

Brenda and her friends stood in a clump while the party raged around them. In her plastic cup was a drink that may have been alcoholic; Brenda couldn't tell by the taste and she was only sipping. On the one hand, they were still in high school. On the other hand, this was a wild Beverly Hills party. Brenda took another sip. Who knew? Asking would have been tacky.

As they passed, a lot of boys looked at Brenda and her friends. Some of the braver ones even said hello. Few of them were real dorks, and many of them were very cute. It was pretty obvious that the main attraction in their group was Kelly.

Michelle felt the bridge of her nose and said, "Maybe I should have *my* bump removed."

Brenda didn't see any bump, but she reflexively felt the bridge of her own nose. Was that a bump?

Kelly said to Brenda, "I had a deviated septum. Rhinoplasty, y'know?"

Michelle and Donna giggled. Even Kelly seemed to be amused. Brenda stared at the middle of Kelly's face. "A nose job? It's beautiful." She tried to imagine what it had looked like before.

Kelly's amusement turned to downright delight. "It is, isn't it? I wish I'd looked like this when I was a freshman."

Over Kelly's shoulder, Brenda saw Brandon and waved. Brandon waved back. The blond guy next to him drank something from a paper bag and looked sullen. All the girls looked in Brandon's direction.

"Who's that?" Kelly asked.

"My brother, Brandon."

"He's really hot," Kelly said, "but he should choose his friends more carefully."

"That's Steve Sanders," Donna said as if it were a secret, and a dirty one at that.

"Who's that?" Brenda said. She thought Steve was cute, but she didn't want to admit it till she knew what was going on.

Kelly said, "My *old* boyfriend. He called me like three hundred times during the summer." She shook her head. "I can't seem to make it clear to him that it's over."

If Kelly could throw away cute guys like that with the garbage, Brenda wondered what the really cute guys were like.

Brandon waved to Brenda, who was conspiring in a corner with the three girls who'd picked her up.

"Who're you waving to?" Steve asked between sips.

"My sister, Brenda. The one with Kelly Taylor."

"Kelly Taylor and her handmaids." Steve made the description sound like an insult. "Some doctor took off about a foot of her nose this summer." He thought about that for a moment and then said, "She used to be my girlfriend before I dumped her." He took a couple of deep breaths.

Brandon was about to ask how Steve would feel if he went over to talk to her, but Steve stalked away. Brandon watched him go. Evidently only Steve's mouth had dumped Kelly Taylor. The rest of him was real angry about something.

Brandon wandered by himself for a while. He didn't exactly go looking for Steve, which was just as well because he didn't find him. It was a big party. Funny how in a crowd this size Brandon could feel so alone. He didn't know anybody, and everybody he saw appeared to be too busy to talk to him—dancing or talking or something. He looked for the brunette he'd unwittingly danced with when he arrived, but he couldn't find her either. He also couldn't find his sister or Kelly Taylor. He might as well have been at a party in Siberia or something.

He stopped, suddenly very tired, and sat in a white wrought-iron chair at a table covered with napkins and empty cups. The other chairs were empty. He shook his head and said to himself, "Time to blow this Popsicle stand."

"If I only could," a nearby female voice said.

Brandon was certain that chair had been empty before. Now it was artistically filled by a slim girl in a clinging knit dress. The shadows of leaves and branches brushed across her, partially hiding her, but Brandon was intrigued by her mouth and chin. And even in the half-light, Brandon could see she had a fantastic figure. Two objects like chandeliers dangled from her ears and flashed what little light there was. She smelled like adventure and mystery and excitement. Hell, she smelled good.

Brandon swallowed and said, "Hi."

"Hi. Want to dance?"

Brandon was not into formal introductions, necessarily, but the girl's question did seem a little abrupt. Still, why not dance? He wasn't, like, busy.

They danced. The band was playing some old-fashioned slow dance number, and the mystery girl clung to Brandon tightly as if he were a life raft. Brandon didn't mind. She felt good against him and her hair smelled more strongly of her musky perfume, but he couldn't help wondering if she'd come with some guy, and how big the guy was, and where that guy was now.

Brandon said, "If you think these parties are bogus, why do you come?"

"I have to come. It's *my* house."

"Your house?" Brandon said in surprise, and

pushed away to look at her.

"Don't do that," she said, and pulled him close again. "You smell good. What is that you're wearing?"

"I don't know," said Brandon. "Tide."

The girl laughed. She had a nice laugh.

Brandon said, "You must be Marianne Moore. I'm Brandon Walsh."

"Very good," Marianne said with a trace of sarcasm.

"So, isn't it kind of weird, like, not enjoying your own party?"

The music continued, but they were barely moving. After a minute Marianne answered, "Maybe it is."

Brandon felt her shiver.

"God knows, my parents always enjoy *their* parties." Marianne shook her head. "But just because I'm popular doesn't mean I have to like everybody." She stopped moving altogether and gently pushed Brandon away. "Nice meeting you, Brandon."

"Can I call you?"

"Sure. Anytime." She whipped out a lipstick from somewhere and used it to write her phone number on Brandon's bare arm in a hot sexy color. "Try not to smear it," she said.

Brandon held his arm away from his body as she walked off across the flagstones. He was hypnotized by the motion of her hips. She had great legs, too. And he could listen to her talk for hours. Brandon was too drunk on love even to wonder why such a girl didn't have a boyfriend.

Kelly was telling Brenda and the others how easy it would be to pretend they were twenty-one and get

into some of the really rad nightclubs. The prospect of
meeting an older man excited Brenda. Then she saw
Steve Sanders walking toward them carefully, as if
afraid he might fall over. The girls stiffened when he
walked up next to Kelly and drank something from the
brown paper bag he carried.

"Hi, Kelly," he said angrily.

Kelly returned a very small "Hi," and tried unsuc-
cessfully to pretend he wasn't there.

"So," Steve said. "Do you want to dance?" His question sounded less like an invitation than a challenge.

"No, thanks. I'm fine right here."

Steve took another drink and worked his hands, making and unmaking fists. He said, "Man, you are so cold."

"Steve, get over it."

Brenda had never before seen a cute guy make
himself as ugly as Steve did when he curled his lip and
said, "Get over *yourself.*"

Steve reeled off, leaving Brenda feeling as if she'd
just witnessed a fight.

Kelly said, "Let's get out of here."

From a safe distance, David Silver and Scott Scott
watched Kelly Taylor. They were both freshmen and a
little uncomfortable being at a party at which they
knew they were not welcome. David, a tall, dark-haired
kid who liked to wear loud Hawaiian shirts, was there
because it was the cool thing to do. Besides, he had a
terrible crush on Kelly. Scott was blond and wore a
Lakers baseball cap wrong side to. He was there
because David was there.

"This is mind-blowing," David said excitedly.
"Another couple hours and I bet some of these girls

start taking their tops off."

"You think?" Scott asked, astonished but intrigued.

"Definitely."

"But my mother's going to pick us up at eleven."

"You go if you want to. If I see flesh, I'm staying."

They watched with some interest when Steve attempted to get Kelly to dance. When Steve stalked away angrily, David grabbed Scott's hat, put it on backward, and hurried after Steve.

Steve was unsteady on his feet. He stopped and rested a hand on the back of a chair while he took another drink from his bag.

David walked up to him and said, "You actually know Kelly Taylor?"

"Yeah, I know her," Steve said. "She's the biggest bitch at West Beverly High. And I should know. I went out with her for a year." Steve looked around to gauge his audience. David drew back a little when Steve began to shout, "I dumped her because she's lousy in bed and she's got a nasty personality."

David nodded and said, "I could live with that."

Steve looked through him for a moment before David registered. "Who are you, anyway?" Steve asked.

They introduced themselves and shook hands.

"Wait a minute!" David exclaimed, "Your mom! She's Samantha Sanders! The mom on *Hartley House*!"

Steve's face took on an expression of disgust. He nodded and fortified himself with another drink.

Apparently, David didn't notice. He rambled on. "I don't believe it! I grew up watching that show in reruns!" He looked off into space, remembering what a great show *Hartley House* was. "I really love your mom. She was like, you know, the perfect mom."

"I hate to break your heart, kid, but my mom ain't

the perfect mom and Kelly Taylor ain't the perfect girl."

Before either of them had a chance to say anything more, a pair of enormous guys approached. The one wearing the Body Glove T-shirt, said, "You're a major waste case, Sanders. Who's driving you home?"

"I am. Leave me alone."

The big guys had other ideas and they scuffled with Steve for a moment. While the one in the T-shirt held him, the other one took the keys from Steve's pocket and said, "You're not driving anywhere tonight, man."

Steve looked around desperately. He pointed to David and said, "He'll drive me home." Steve grabbed back his keys and thrust them into David's hand. David stared from Steve to the keys in disbelief. Quickly, Steve threw an arm across his shoulder and walked him away.

When they reached the driveway David saw Steve's black Corvette and said, "Oh, my God." He dumped Steve into the passenger seat, then ran around to the other side of the car. As he put the key into the ignition, he turned to Steve and said, "I have to tell you, man. I don't have a license."

Steve had been counting his fingers. He looked at David blankly and laughed like an idiot.

David started the car. It growled like a hundred happy lions. He ground it into first gear and slowly moved away from the curb. When he eased the car into second, it leaped ahead and his cap flew off. David hunkered down and kept driving. He asked Steve where he lived.

"Four-two-oh-three Doheny Road," Steve said, and laughed again.

The ride was not smooth. A few times they attracted the attention of the Beverly Hills police, but each
time David smiled and waved and managed to prod
Steve into sitting up straight and looking like a normal
passenger. At a stoplight, Kelly and her friends came
up next to the 'vette in a red BMW. One of the girls
cried out, "Steve! Some geek is driving your car!" Steve
just laughed and waved and went back to sleep. He
snored loudly.

David found the address and pulled into the dark-
ened driveway of a sprawling ranch-style house—not
large by Marianne Moore standards, but comfy. David
jimmied Steve out of the passenger bucket and half
carried him to the front door. Steve kept saying he
would never forget his good buddy David, and David
kept reassuring him that it had been no problem.
Finally David watched Steve stumble into the house
and close the door.

As he turned around David dusted off his hands,
then suddenly froze. The Corvette was rolling backward down the driveway. It picked up speed and rolled
into the street. It rolled backward across the street and
crashed into a parked Mercedes. Glass tinkled.

The entire side door of the Mercedes was a ruin.
The rear of the Corvette looked like a crumpled shopping bag. Lights went on in the house behind the
Mercedes. David looked over his shoulder but there
was no sign of life in the Sanders house.

He looked back at the wreckage, rocked for a few
seconds, and then ran very fast down the middle of the
street. Soon he was out of sight in the darkness where
the streetlights did not reach.

3

If you remember the party, you weren't there

STEVE PRESENTED THE DESTROYED BACK END of his Corvette to Brandon as if it were some kind of parlor trick. Brandon studied the damage and listened to Steve tell how it happened as far as he could remember, then shook his head in sympathy. Radios all around them blared KWBH, the school station. While Steve ranted on about his car, the Flash broke in with an announcement: "I hear Friday night's party at Marianne Moore's house was a real blast. And though we're only one week into the new semester, we already have a contender for the Flashman of the Year. The ossified Steve Sanders. Remember much, Steve?"

Music began again and Steve angrily flipped off the radio. It was a useless gesture, because the music continued from car radios all around him.

"Comedian," Steve grumbled.

"Tough," Brandon said.

"Look, do you have any idea who drove me home from that party?"

"You don't remember?"

"Don't start with me, Walsh," Steve said angrily.

"Whoa there, I'm on *your* side, remember?"

"Yeah. Sorry. I don't know who drove me home. When I find him, I'm going to kill him. Is that clear enough for everybody?"

Throughout the day, David wore a big hat and dark glasses. During lunch he told Scott what had happened and said for the hundredth time, "He's going to kill me. I'm going to die." He didn't even sound worried. Evidently, death at the hands of Steve Sanders had become a fact of life, like pop quizzes.

At another table in the cafeteria, Kelly was putting the final touches on Brenda's Minnesota driver's license while Donna and Brenda watched. During chemistry, Kelly had began to modify the birth year so that Brenda would appear to be twenty-one. She didn't get a chance to finish because Mr. Ridley insisted they pay attention to the lesson.

Now Kelly lifted her pencil and appraised her work. "I am such an artist," she said as she passed the license across the table.

Brenda took the driver's license and stared at it in awe. There was no doubt that Kelly did beautiful work. But Brenda was still worried. She said, "Do you think anybody will buy this?"

"Absolutely," Kelly said. She took up a lettuce leaf

and nibbled on the edge. "First of all, nobody in Los Angeles knows what a Minnesota driver's license looks like. And anyway, I think getting in really depends on whether the doorman thinks you're cute."

Brenda frowned.

"Trust me," said Donna, "you're cute."

Brenda shook her head.

"What?" said Kelly. "You don't like my work?"

"Your work is totally awesome. But I thought trying to get into a club if you're under age is against the law. I've never broken a law before." Brenda was aware that Kelly and Donna were watching her, evaluating her, and she was somehow coming up short. Her friendship with them could expire in a cloud of misplaced virtue. High school would be a total loss. She worked up a chuckle and said, "God, I'm such a wuss."

Donna said, "The worst that can happen is that they don't let you in."

Brenda flashed on a women-behind-bars movie she'd seen once. In it, the pretty, but wrongly convicted woman was attacked with a rubber hose by a matron who was built like a linebacker. The screams had given Brenda nightmares for weeks. Of course, she'd been very young then. Besides, she reminded herself, it was *only a movie*. With an enthusiasm she did not entirely feel, Brenda said, "So, when do we road-test this baby?"

Kelly nodded and smiled. Brenda felt better already. Kelly said, "Saturday night. The Blue Iguana. Are we there?"

"Definitely," Brenda and Donna said together.

Brandon looked all over for Marianne, and he

found her at last in what he considered an unlikely spot. She had staked out a picnic table under a tree at the far side of campus. While not the femme fatale she'd been at her party, she still looked very cute in her tight, fashionably ripped jeans and Cure T-shirt. She bobbed her head in time with the music she was listening to through earphones. When she saw Brandon, she took off the earphones and said, "Hi."

"Hi," Brandon said. "Great party the other night."

"The great bogus bash? I thought you had a lousy time."

Brandon smiled, but deep inside he wondered if he had enough charm to carry off what he had in mind. He said, "No. I meant the part where I met you."

"Oh," Marianne said, and poked a box of sushi with chopsticks.

Brandon sat down across from her and said, "Listen. Would you like to go to Paris for the weekend? If we leave Friday night, I think we can make it back late Monday morning—only have to miss two classes."

Marianne didn't even seem surprised. But she did seem interested, which was all Brandon wanted. She said, "Seriously?"

Brandon had not expected that question. Did she really believe *everybody* had as much money as her parents? He said, "Uh, no. Not seriously."

Marianne crawled further into the idea. "We could do it, you know." Brandon blinked and pursed his lips. This was getting way out of hand. Marianne said, "I mean, it *is* possible."

Brandon thought very fast. This was not going the way he'd planned at all. Not even his parents would consider going to Paris for the weekend. If *he* tried it, he'd be paying off his allowance into the next century.

He knew he had to come clean before it was too late. "Trust me, I was only kidding. Really. We can do Paris another weekend. This weekend we could go somewhere more local. You know, somewhere we could go to and come back from on Saturday night. We could start around eight o'clock, maybe?"

Brandon liked the smile on Marianne's face. It wasn't the hard fake thing she'd used at the party. It seemed to be more natural and to have some warmth behind it. He was almost lost in it when Marianne answered, "Sounds great. You know where I live."

Suddenly Brandon felt nervous and excited and wonderful. Things fizzed all through his body. He backed off, clapping and washing his hands. "Excellent. See you then."

He waved and walked away without any idea of where in the world he could take a girl like Marianne, a place where she wouldn't be bored out of her mind. It occurred to him who might have the answer to a tricky social question like this.

So preoccupied with Marianne was he, that Brandon didn't know how he got to the *Blaze* newsroom. But once inside, he found the entire staff typing madly. Andrea looked up at him from her computer and raised one eyebrow.

Brandon leaned at her over her computer and said, "Do you know any good places to go for dinner? Like someplace romantic? Like on a Saturday night?"

Andrea sat up a little straighter and she opened her mouth into a small *oh*, making her look very cute indeed. Brandon got the impression that this was not just another question for Andrea. Was it possible that she thought he was asking *her* for a date?

Andrea asked, "Is she someone special?"

"I don't know. She could be."

Andrea blushed.

Wrong! Brandon thought. Wrong! He looked for a way to change the subject. He grabbed the one nearest at hand and said, "So, why weren't you at Marianne Moore's party the other night?"

Andrea adjusted her glasses. Brandon was relieved to see that she was cool once again, the complete professional. She said, "Hanging out with a bunch of people acting stupid isn't going to get me into an Ivy League school."

Brandon shook his head. "Isn't there anything for you besides school?"

"Who's got the time? I also do ten hours a week of community service." She hugged herself. "The Ivys love stuff like that."

"Sure. Well, *hasta luego*." Brandon headed for the door, feeling as if he'd escaped some terrible trap.

Andrea called after him, "Moonshadows."

Brandon turned around and said, "What?"

"It's a restaurant on the beach in Malibu. Real romantic."

"Thanks, Andrea. I knew you'd know stuff like that."

Brenda's preparations for Saturday night began long before the actual assault on the Blue Iguana. She pulled out all the makeup she owned and looked at it critically. Boxes, bottles, tubes, and jars stood in confusion on the bathroom counter looking like either the Emerald City of Oz or the result of a tornado at the Robinson's cosmetic counter. She'd purchased all this stuff in Minneapolis, but that couldn't be helped.

She made her first selection and began. She didn't like what she saw, got all of it off with tissue and cold cream, and began again. That was better. She applied layer after layer of color.

When her mother came in to check up on her, Mrs. Walsh seemed equally curious and horrified by what Brenda was doing. Brenda tried to explain that this was Beverly Hills and you had to be more glamorous than kids were in Minneapolis. When Mrs. Walsh still seemed unsure of the necessity or wisdom of what Brenda was doing, Brenda offered to loan her any of the makeup she wanted to try.

In the mirror, Mrs. Walsh gauged the effect of a little blusher.

Brenda gave her face a final dab, fluffed her hair one last time, and grabbed her coat. She ran from the bedroom, not an easy thing to do in the high heels she was wearing.

Mrs. Walsh called down the stairs after her, "Home by twelve! I'm serious!"

Without stopping, Brenda called over her shoulder, "Twelve forty-five!"

"Twelve-fifteen!"

Her mom's final bid was cut off by the slamming of the front door. Brenda took a deep breath of the silky night air they used only in Beverly Hills. Somebody startled her by opening the front door and racing past her toward Mondale. It was Brandon, looking very nice in a sport coat and slacks. Not hip, but nice. The truth was, Brandon had never been as hip as she was.

Brenda said, "Where are you going?"

Brandon turned and said, "I have a date."

"With who?"

Brandon seemed to hesitate for a moment. When

he told her, she knew why. Marianne Moore was famous, or maybe infamous. She was the hostess with the mostest, and she liked to spread it around. Brenda said, "I hear she got arrested for going topless at Zuma Beach last summer."

A car horn blasted through the still night air. It was Kelly and Donna. Brenda waved.

Brandon said, "I bet you got that from those stuck-up friends of yours."

"You're just jealous because I *have* some friends. This isn't Minneapolis, Brandon. I told you. You have to work at it."

"Who died and made you Dear Abby? You didn't have a friend in Minneapolis who wasn't my friend first."

"That's a lie and you know it."

Kelly honked again and cried, "Come on, *Brenda!*"

Brenda gave Brandon a final dirty look and ran as best she could for Kelly's BMW. Her skirt was very short and she had to be careful getting into the car.

Kelly, Donna, and Brenda all agreed that they looked very hot indeed. "They might not even card us," Kelly said. Brenda thought this was unlikely. "Remember," Kelly went on, "passing for twenty-one is all attitude."

Brenda didn't know anyone who was twenty-one. She briefly considered acting like her mother, who was considerably older than twenty-one, then decided that her mother was perhaps *too* mature. If she were to show up at the Blue Iguana, the doorman might not let her in because of insufficient hipness.

Kelly entrusted the BMW to a uniformed attendant who gave them the once-over and smiled. "Have a good time, ladies," he said before he got into the car and drove away.

"He called us *ladies*," Donna said excitedly.

"We are definitely stylin' now," Kelly said.

The Blue Iguana was a large white building with a blue neon iguana twitching its tail above a single black door. The door was guarded by a big, muscular guy wearing wraparound shades and a very nice coat with the collar turned up. He seemed to be carding everybody, even kids who were obviously in college. Every time the door opened, wild, hip music escaped.

Brenda drew confidence from Kelly, who successfully gave the impression that she'd been in this dive before and was doing them a favor by coming back. Brenda thought they sounded very sharp as their high heels clicked against the sidewalk. They looked sharp, too. Their attitude was in the mid-twenties. They were *stylin'*, as Kelly had said. How could they not get in?

Kelly put her hand on the door and the doorman asked to see some ID.

"Give me a break," Donna said with disgust, and rolled her eyes. Brenda thought she was overdoing the act just a little.

The doorman just held out his hand and smiled.

Brenda had her Minnesota driver's license out first. Trying not to show her nervousness, she handed it over. It seemed to immediately shrink in the guy's enormous fist. He lifted his shades and glanced from the license to Brenda and then back. The music roared in Brenda's ears. She could feel her heart beating. If attitude was everything, she was in big trouble. She felt as if she were wearing diapers.

The doorman handed back the license and said, "Okay. You're in."

With an incredible sense of relief and expectation,

Brenda took the license back, waved at her friends, and ducked inside as the doorman took Kelly's card.

She stopped just inside the door. The place was a huge, dark barn. Lights flashed on the walls and on the ceiling. More neon iguanas in different colors were everywhere. The place smelled of perfume and beer, and loud music played in another room. She stepped forward as her eyes got used to the darkness, and she could see people gyrating to the music. The crowd around the bar was at least three deep.

She waited under a pink iguana, where she had a good view of the door. People came in and spread out. None of them were her friends. She waited a long time and they never came in.

Brenda felt abandoned and more than a little frightened. Was this some weird Beverly Hills hazing rite? Brenda decided to give her friends the benefit of the doubt. The doorman just wouldn't let them in. So, without meaning to, *she* had abandoned *them*. Still, it seemed a real waste for her to leave so soon. Kelly would certainly want her to go for it now that she was inside. Yet what would she do in a place like this all by herself?

4

When you're hot, you're hot

WHEN BRANDON ARRIVED AT MARIANNE'S house, she managed to surprise him again. Instead of wearing some short, hot number like Brenda and her friends wore to parties, she wore a leather jumpsuit covered with buckles, zippers, and snaps. It was tight and shiny and she looked awesome in it.

Marianne took them to Moonshadows on her Harley-Davidson. Aside from the fact that she insisted they both wear helmets—"Don't want to ruin my makeup if there's an accident," she said—she seemed to take a lot of chances. Brandon arrived at the restaurant windblown and exhilarated.

Moonshadows was a great success. The ride on the Harley made Brandon very hungry. He and Marianne fed each other scampi, letting the melted butter drip all over their faces. The sexual tension hung so thick in the air, you could cut it with a fork.

When it was time to go home, Marianne insisted that Brandon drive. She refused to listen to his protest that he'd never before driven a motorcycle, let alone a Harley-Davidson. As it turned out, he was pretty good at it. Except for that one moment when Marianne had tried to dive into his ear tongue first.

Brandon didn't know what to expect when they returned to Marianne's house—anything from a handshake and a peck on the cheek to a suggestion that he engage in activities he'd never even dreamed of. The reality turned out to be somewhere in between.

Marianne found him a bathing suit and sent him out to a cabana to change. When Brandon emerged, he found her waiting for him. She wore a red one-piece spandex bathing suit that left very little to Brandon's imagination. She was so beautiful, it was scary.

She took his hand and led him to a hot tub from which they could look down on the sparkling city. As they slowly cooked in the bubbling water, French rock-and-roll songs played to them over loudspeakers. Marianne closed her eyes and sang along softly. Brandon wanted to enjoy himself, but everything was moving too fast. He sat stiffly in the water, willing his heart to beat more slowly and wishing that he'd taken French instead of Spanish.

Marianne stopped singing. She opened her eyes, leaned across the tub, and kissed Brandon on the cheek. Brandon smiled, but otherwise did not respond.

Marianne said, "I think you're really nice."

"I think you're really nice, too." Dumb. Repeating what she said was dumb.

Marianne kissed Brandon again, this time hard on the mouth. He had trouble breathing, but he didn't fight her. Suddenly she pulled away from him and leered at him wickedly, invitingly. She said, "Let's take off all our clothes." Then, watching Brandon closely, she began to slowly slide her shoulder straps down her arms. Brandon grabbed her hands.

"What's wrong?" Marianne asked, surprised.

"Didn't your mother tell you about playing hard to get?"

Marianne laughed while she shook her head. She said, "*My* mother? She probably thinks I'm a prude."

"Huh?"

"Brandon, my dad manages rock bands. He met my mom on the road. She was this major groupie. They did things that would blow you away. I mean, they think my life is a total bore."

"What do *you* think of your life?"

Marianne slid the straps of her bathing suit back into place and looked into the water. "I just feel so trapped sometimes. When I go out and have fun, everyone calls me a party girl. Then when I want to be left alone or act quiet, they call me stuck-up." She looked at him. "I can't win."

Brandon edged over and put his arm around her. She went rigid, and then relaxed into him. He shook his head and said, "Years from now I'm going to look back on this night and kick myself for being such an idiot."

Marianne kissed him chastely on the cheek. "No, you won't," she said. " I won't let you."

Silently, they watched the city sparkle beneath them.

Brenda couldn't make the manager understand that her friends were outside and that he must let them in. She turned away from him in despair and was on the point of leaving—the logical thing to do—when some guy walked up to her. He was older than a high-school senior and dressed a little conservatively for the Blue Iguana. But he was neat and clean, not a weirdo. And he was very cute. He said, "What's the problem?" and looked at her with some concern.

Here was this handsome older man giving her the perfect opening. What should she say? For some reason he terrified her. Maybe it was because he was this handsome older man. She said, "Uh, it's nothing. My friends ditched me." She shrugged.

"That sucks," he said, oozing sincerity. "Can I buy you a drink or something?"

"Uh, no. I better call my mo—" Bad move. "A cab. I better call a cab."

A waitress appeared from out of the darkness. She was a blonde. Like all the waitresses, she wore black tights and a man's white silk shirt. The stranger didn't seem to notice that she was very attractive. He had eyes only for Brenda. At his urging, she ordered a drink, a banana daiquiri, something she'd heard her mom order once. While the waitress went to get their drinks, they introduced themselves. His name was Jason.

They sat down at a tiny round table and Jason asked, "Are you in school?"

"Yes," Brenda said, taking a chance. "UCLA."

"Groovy. That's where I went to law school. Are you with a sorority? I know all of them at UCLA."

Oops. She'd never be able to keep this up. Besides, nobody said *groovy* anymore. Maybe he was *too* old. Still, he was *very* cute. And he seemed nice. Brenda reached wildly for an answer to Jason's question. She said, "It's a new sorority. We all just transferred from Minnesota."

"The whole house? How weird."

The drinks arrived and Brenda sipped hers. It was sweet and foamy and tasted like bananas. While she sipped, Brenda tried to think up a new subject. They talked for a while, Brenda more or less successfully keeping up her end. The more she drank, the more difficult thinking became. Even so, the lies she told as she went on became more complicated. Jason never caught her, or never admitted he caught her, anyway.

Brenda had two banana daiquiris, mostly because sipping gave her time to think when she had to answer a question. Maybe it was the drinks that agreed to have a look when Jason asked if she would like to see his condo.

Things moved very quickly after that. When they arrived at the condo, he kissed her, which was nice, and then he began to unbutton her blouse, which frightened her more than anything a boy had ever done. She put her hands on his and he stopped. "No, Jason. I can't," she said as she readjusted her clothes.

He seemed surprised. "Why not?"

"I just can't."

He told her how much he respected her, and when she asked him to take her home, he nodded. Of course, Brenda had to direct him to UCLA's sorority row, which was inconvenient, but she saw no alternative, other than fessing up to everything.

"There it is," Brenda said, and pointed vaguely.

"I think that's a church," Jason said.

"The next one."

Jason gave her his phone number, and once more

they acknowledged it was too bad she did not have a phone of her own.

"Sorry you couldn't spend the night."

Brenda bit her lip and then stopped. She said, "Me too," and dashed from the car. She sauntered up the walk to the imposing stone building she'd claimed was her sorority house, hoping he'd get tired of watching and drive away. She was almost to the door and planned to fumble for her keys for as long as it took, when she heard his car pull away and her shoulders sagged with relief.

The walk to a gas station seemed to be long, but she found one at last. The attendant was a college kid about Jason's age. He eyed her openly as she used the pay phone to call a cab. She regretted wearing such a short dress.

The cab came and took her home. It was a good thing she had an emergency stash or she never would have been able to pay the driver. She sighed with relief when she took off her shoes and went inside the house.

As she was skulking up the stairs, someone grabbed her from behind. She yelped. It was Brandon, also with his shoes in his hand.

Brandon whispered. "What are you doing home so late?"

"None of your beeswax. What are you doing home so late?"

"None of your beeswax."

They glared at each other for a moment, then both said at once, "Don't tell Mom." That made them smile, which made Brenda feel better. They went to their rooms.

Brenda took off her clothes and put on a flannel

night gown, which felt warm and comfy after her tight party clothes. She was so tired, she considered sleeping in her makeup, but remembered an article she'd once read about taking care of your complexion. It would be just her luck to wake up with her face looking like a connect-the-dots puzzle. Even so, she decided that this once it wouldn't matter, and she fell into bed with her makeup on anyway.

She lay there with her eyes closed, but she was too wired to sleep. Jason kept floating through her thoughts with his hand on the buttons of her blouse. Had she done the right thing? Would she ever have another chance to sleep with a handsome, older man? She listened to the house creak as she tossed and turned.

When gray light came in through her window, she looked at the bedside clock. Six. Early, but it would have to be late enough. She could no longer stand keeping her adventures to herself. She had to tell somebody what had happened the night before. She had to get advice. She called Kelly.

When Kelly came on the line, she sounded half-asleep. But she perked right up when Brenda said, "I met a guy."

"In the Blue Iguana? The jerk at the door wouldn't even let us in!"

"His name is Jason and he's twenty-five and he's a lawyer. And he's so cute."

"You slept with him?"

"No. But he wanted me to."

Brenda expected a comment on that, but Kelly was strangely silent. Through the phone, Brenda heard another voice, seemingly coming from across the room. "Kelly! Who is that?"

"Just a friend, Mom."

The other voice belonged to Kelly's mom, Jackie. Jackie had to be the hippest mom on the planet. She and Kelly shared wardrobes, and they *both* looked good. Brenda could still hear voices, but they were muffled, as if Kelly had put her hand over the phone's mouthpiece.

Kelly came back and said, "Still there?"

"Yeah. Kelly, he thinks I'm in college. What am I going to do?"

"Have a good time. That's what I always do."

"You've gone out with college men?" Brenda cried.

Kelly admitted that she had, but refused to talk about it over the phone at six in the morning. "We'll talk at school," she said.

Before the bell, Brandon sat in Spanish class trying to keep his mind on his tenses and not on Ms. Montes. He mumbled, "'I must have been fishing, they must have been fishing, we all must have been—'" He was interrupted by the arrival of Steve, who threw down his books on the desk and leaned close to Brandon. "I was talking to Kelly, this morning and—"

"And *Kelly* talked to *you*?" He looked at Steve with amazement.

"Lighten up, Walsh. Kelly saw the dorkmeier who drove me home from Marianne Moore's party. She says he looked like a freshman."

"That's a clue," Brandon said. "Only three hundred or so male freshmen at West Beverly."

"I'm going to talk to every one of them," Steve said with determination. "And when I find the guy, I'm going to kill him."

The bell rang then, and at the same moment a delivery guy came into the room with a very fancy bouquet of flowers, mostly roses.

To Brandon's astonishment, the flowers were for him. The other kids in class laughed and made rude remarks. When Brandon sat down with the flowers, not knowing quite what to do with them, Steve yanked away the card and read it. He looked at Brandon with new respect. "These are from Marianne Moore. Man, you must have been awesome!"

Evidently Marianne had thought so too, though Brandon was certain that Steve's definition of awesome was very different from Marianne's.

But that was nobody's business. Brandon just smiled with contentment and said, "Yeah."

5

Wild things

DAVID SILVER AND SCOTT SCOTT SAT ON THE lunch court trying to appear inconspicuous. David still wore a big floppy hat and wraparound shades. Every time somebody passed, he ducked.

Scott said, "If he hasn't nailed you by now, bro, he probably won't."

"You think?"

Scott shrugged, but said, "Definitely. And I want my Lakers cap back."

David snapped his fingers and said, "Uh, I forgot it at home again."

"I bet you lost it."

"I didn't lose it."

"Then where is it?"

David worked his mouth for a moment. He looked across the school yard, then said, "In Steve Sanders's

Corvette." He flinched.

Scott grabbed David by the arm and said very seriously, "David, that hat had my name sewn into it."

"Hey, dudes."

David and Scott looked up at the person who had spoken. It was Steve Sanders. He shoved a piece of paper into each of their hands, fliers. The fliers were both the same and showed a stick figure of a person with the word DORK written boldly across the head. Next to it was a picture of Steve's crumpled 'vette.

Steve said, "Fifty bucks for the guy who helps me nail the terrorist who drove me home after Marianne Moore's party." He walked off, but neither David nor Scott saw where he went. They were too busy contemplating the fliers in their hands.

"We're both history," Scott said.

David said nothing, but shook his head slowly.

Brandon attracted a lot of attention carrying the flowers around school. He felt a little nervous about it, first, because he was ordinarily a pretty private kind of guy, and second, because he knew that all those leering faces had the wrong idea about him and Marianne. Still, being a very heavy dude on campus was certainly a nice change from being the little man who wasn't there. It made him feel good, and Brandon could not quite bring himself to correct anybody's perceptions.

In the *Blaze* office, Brandon dumped pencils from a mayonnaise jar he'd brought from home and stood up the flowers in it. He was looking at them and thinking about Marianne when Andrea came in, nodded in his direction, and went to her desk.

Brandon sat down in the chair next to Andrea's

desk and handed her a rose. "Thanks for the suggestion," he said. "Moonshadows was totally tubular."

She took the rose but did not sniff it. Instead, she regarded Brandon for a moment and then said, "Funny, I don't see the two of you as a couple."

"Why not?"

"I don't know," Andrea said. "You seem so smart and sensible. Marianne is more kind of, how you say, stupid and excessive."

Brandon shook his head. "That's not true at all."

"Okay. Tell me about the *real* Marianne Moore."

Somehow, this had stopped being a friendly conversation and had become an interview. Brandon wondered if everything he said was going to turn up in the paper. Probably not. Sensationalism wasn't Andrea's style. Brandon said, "I don't know. But she's got this image that's not really her. And then guys go out with her expecting stuff, and after a while she just feels obligated to deliver. Does that make sense?"

Andrea nodded, seemingly impressed. She said, "Maybe you should be writing our advice column." She handed back the rose and said, "Thanks anyway, but I'm..." She grabbed for a handful of tissues and sneezed. "I'm allergic to roses."

Brandon strolled back to his desk. He turned and shook the single rose in Andrea's direction as if it symbolized something they should both remember.

Later, while he walked through the halls, a lot of guys congratulated him and slapped him on the back. Girls just pointed and giggled. He was suddenly everybody's friend.

An enormous guy who was in his gym class came over and slapped the flat of his hand against Brandon's locker, preventing him from opening it. DeWitt said,

"Marianne Moore sent you flowers?"

Brandon smiled nervously. He said, "I wouldn't call them flowers, exactly."

DeWitt laughed, called Brandon "my man," and gave him the thumbs-up. It was like that all day. After a while, the rumors of what Brandon and Marianne had done together grew more wild and specific. Brandon didn't even know what some of the words meant.

As the adulation continued Brandon became more uneasy. After all, he was being congratulated for things he hadn't done. And hadn't he become popular for all the wrong reasons, just like Marianne? He took comfort in the fact that *he* at any rate wasn't spreading rumors.

And popularity was popularity; he couldn't see that it was hurting anybody. Having friends for a change was nice.

During breakfast the next morning, Brenda didn't say a word to Brandon except for "Please pass the butter." On the way to school, she might as well have been an iceberg in the bucket seat next to him. Soon she could no longer contain herself, and she blurted out, "I heard about you and Marianne Moore."

Brandon glanced at her. Why was she so angry? He shook his head and laughed. "From who?"

"Brandon, it's all over the school!"

"Yeah yeah. Sure sure."

As they approached the school and the KWBH signal became stronger, Brandon discovered that Brenda was correct. The people who'd spoken to him about The Date were not isolated cases. Just about all the Flash talked about were those new West Beverly High Wild Things, Brandon Walsh and Marianne Moore. When Brandon pulled into a parking place, Brenda leaped from the car as quickly as she could. Brandon could not blame her. This whole thing had gotten way out of hand. What had been a private Saturday-night date now had acquired the notoriety of an MTV video.

Wherever Brandon went, guys gave him the high-five and girls watched him with admiration, disgust, or speculation. He felt like a celebrity, and it was fun, even if he really didn't deserve all the attention.

He rounded a corner and saw a figure coming toward him from the far end of the rapidly clearing hallway. It was Marianne. And for reasons he could not properly explain, even to himself, he did not want to talk to her. He wanted to run, but he felt trapped by her unwavering gaze.

6

When you're not, you're not

SHE DID NOT LOOK ANGRY, BRANDON thought. She did not look anything. But she kept coming, and the longer he waited, the more unavoidable was their meeting.

"Hi, Marianne," Brandon said.

Marianne said nothing, but punched him hard in the stomach, knocking all the wind out of him. He was more surprised than hurt. While he regained his breath, she said, "You're just like every other creep. You used me to make a name for yourself." She sounded angry and on the edge of tears.

Brandon didn't get it. He continued to gasp while he said, "I swear, I didn't say anything!"

"If you didn't, then who did?"

Brandon tried to speak, but Marianne wouldn't let him. She said, "I really thought I could trust you,

Brandon. I didn't want anything more from you than to have a friend in this school. A *real* friend. I thought you could use one of those yourself."

Brandon leaned against the wall, still recovering. Where had this all come from? How could his innocent increase in popularity suddenly have turned so sour? Disoriented, bewildered by Marianne's verbal assault, he said, "I did. I mean, I do." This was all wrong.

While Brandon searched for something to say that would repair everything, Marianne spoke as if to herself. The fire had gone out of her. She was merely describing her place in the universe. She said, "They probably wouldn't have believed the truth, anyway."

Brandon turned to watch as she slowly walked away. She was still a pretty girl. He still liked her. But the tension between them now had less to do with sex than with misunderstandings, lost chances, and blown friendships. Something needed to be done. Marianne turned and studied Brandon for a moment before she said, "See you at the next big party." She shrugged. "It'll probably be at my house."

As she continued down the empty hall Brandon wondered again what he had done wrong, and what he could do to fix it.

Throughout the day, Brandon replayed the scene with Marianne in his head over and over. He had to do something. After his confrontation with Marianne, his life quickly lost altitude. Some guys still slapped him on the back and some girls still leered at him through lazy eyes, but Brenda avoided him, and in Spanish, Andrea belabored him with a Spanish phrase he didn't understand. But it seemed to impress Ms. Montes, and she nearly spit at him when she translated. Evidently, Andrea had called him a stupid pig.

Brandon felt as if he deserved it, but not knowing why was driving him crazy.

Spanish class dragged on. Suddenly it was interrupted by a loud beeping noise. Steve Sanders swore under his breath and pulled a flat plastic case from his pocket. He turned off the alarm, and while Brandon and Ms. Montes and the others watched with astonishment he ran to the window and leaped out.

Ms. Montes didn't even try to control the class as the students quickly collected around the windows and watched Steve run toward his car, crying, "You guys are dead meat!" at the two geeks who were rummaging around inside it. The taller, less blond of the two geeks ran away, but Steve roughly pulled the other from inside his car, turned off the master alarm, and, having a good grip on the geek's shirtfront, slammed him against the hood. He clutched a Lakers cap in one fist and he cringed as if Steve were beating him.

"You're the guy who drove me home," Steve cried in triumph.

"No!" the geek cried hysterically. "No! I swear I wasn't!"

By this time the one who'd escaped had come back and stood on the other side of the car. Calmly he said, "That's the wrong guy, you jerk. I drove you home."

Steve studied the tall geek, and let go of the blond, who was whimpering.

"Remember?" said the tall one. "I told you I was a fan of your mom's."

If Brandon was any judge, he saw dawn come up behind Steve's eyes. Like a wrestler, Steve sidestepped to the end of his car. He never took his eyes off the tall geek.

The tall geek moved to put the car between them

again and said, "You were too wasted to drive. I did you a favor, man."

Steve and the geek continued to circle the car, but Brandon could tell from his voice that Steve was considering what the geek had said. "So what happened?"

"After I dropped you off, I forgot to put your car in gear. I'm not used to driving a stick."

Steve stood his ground and shook his head.

The geek went on, "I admit it. It was my fault. I may have to work at McDonald's for the rest of my life, but somehow I'll pay to have your car fixed."

Steve said, "I have insurance, you moron."

Brandon knew that calling somebody a moron was just standard Steve Sanders abuse. The guy was safe now, at least from physical harm. Steve walked back toward the classroom building grumbling to himself.

The tall mouthy geek called after him, "Hey, see you at the next party!" Brandon couldn't figure out whether the guy was not awfully bright, or whether he was just so stoked on talking to a guy like Steve that he'd forgotten how close he'd come to death. The blond kid looked at his friend with amazement and admiration.

Everybody watched Steve climb back in through the classroom window. Like Brandon, almost every one of them had a copy of Steve's flier and had heard his "dead meat" speech. Steve said, "So I let him live. I was feeling benevolent, okay?" He threw himself into his seat and slid down until his neck touched the backrest.

Brandon wondered if he could solve his problem with Marianne as easily as Steve had solved his problem with his car. Probably not.

■ ■ ■

Brenda had called Jason at his office, and they'd made a date for that evening. It was a school night, but Brenda felt that only a *kid* would use that as an excuse for postponing a social engagement.

She was standing in front of the mirror in her room combing out her hair, and practicing how to say hello like an adult. She just couldn't get it right. Brenda was such a wuss name.

She jumped when Brandon said, "Hey, Bren. Can we talk for a second?" He was standing in her doorway.

Think adult, Brenda thought. Think composed and collected. Don't let him see he surprised you. She said, "About what?" She continued to run the comb through her hair.

"Don't you miss Minneapolis?"

Brenda put down the comb and folded her hair up against the back of her head. Was she sophisticated or what? She continued to experiment with hairstyles while she said, "Brandon, I really don't have time for a trip down memory lane right now. I have a date."

"On a Tuesday? With who?"

Brandon was such a child. Brenda said, "He's in college, but if you tell Mom, I'll kill you."

Brandon held up open palms and said, "I won't say a word, I swear."

Brandon didn't say anything for a long time and Brenda thought he'd given up and gone away. He startled her again when he said, "Listen: I want to ask you about that rumor going around about me and Marianne. I don't know, I feel responsible, like I started it somehow because I never really denied it."

Brenda didn't have time for Brandon's moonings. She had to get dressed. She told him it would blow over as she shooed him from the room and closed the door.

She dragged out all her formal clothes, all the stuff she'd rejected when going to Blue Iguana—she couldn't wear the same thing for Jason twice, after all—and threw them onto her bed. After long deliberation, she chose a red top with matching skirt. It would look great with her black jacket and black heels. She ran out of hairspray while teasing her hair into a proper mane and had to borrow some of her mom's.

The family was eating dinner when she walked into the kitchen to say good-night, and she got the usual inquisition from her parents. Brandon just stared.

As Brenda rushed across the room, her father called, "Back by ten!"

"Ten-thirty," Brenda called as she opened the door.

"Ten-fifteen!"

Brenda had heard her father say ten-fifteen, but she could safely pretend that she hadn't because the door slammed right on his words. As she walked down the driveway she forgot about her family and fantasized about what a heavenly night it was going to be.

7

A lot of talk

THE PLACE WAS CALLED ENYART'S, AND IT WAS very posh. The walls were pink, and gray air-conditioning ducts ran across the ceiling like big trendy snakes.

Brenda had hoped that she would have Jason all to herself, but he'd invited another couple, Alison and Ron. Ron worked in Jason's law office, and Alison was his girlfriend, a tall, thin, nervous woman with unexceptional hair. The three of them wore jeans and sweaters. Brenda was a little overdressed, but that was good, wasn't it?

The four of them sat shoulder to shoulder around a small table while they ate pasta and drank wine. Brenda had no idea if the wine was any good, but Jason ordered an additional bottle, so it must have been at least all right. When Ron asked what her college major was, Brenda said the first thing that came into her mind.

"Astronomy," Alison repeated, impressed. "You didn't tell us she was a brain, Jason."

"First I hear of it," Jason said, and squeezed Brenda's hand under the table. Brenda knew she was blushing, but maybe in the dim light nobody would notice. She squeezed back.

Ron said, "This is my big chance to find something out. I mean, what is a black hole, *really*?"

Brenda felt as if she were falling into one. Really. Why did she have to say *astronomy*? Why did anybody find that interesting? She smiled bravely and, making it up as she want along, said, "Well, I guess the easiest way to explain it, without a working knowledge of, uh, fourth-dimensional geometry, is that it's like, well, a hole. In space."

After a short silence—during which everyone at the table considered Brenda's explanation, and Brenda wished she were somewhere else, alone with Jason—Ron said, "I still don't get it."

Jason and Alison groaned, and Brenda thought it might be okay to laugh good-naturedly, so she tried it to good effect.

Ron was about to say something else, but Alison beat him to it. She said, "Jason tells us your entire sorority house transferred from Minnesota."

Why are we talking about me? Brenda wondered. She said, "Well, not exactly. Just five of us, really."

"I told you, Jason," Alison said. "It couldn't be the entire house."

"That's what she said," Jason said.

Another big laugh. After that the talk turned to college football and other things. Brenda didn't know much about them, but smiling and nodding seemed to be all that was required of her.

Later, the evening got much more interesting. Jason drove her back to the building she'd claimed was her sorority house, and they got into some very heavy necking. He wanted her to stay over the following weekend. "Tell your housemother you're, I don't know, visiting your parents or something."

The word *parents* sent an electric shock through Brenda. She was aware that this was a moment of truth. She sidestepped it by saying, "I'll try."

"Try hard," Jason said. Brenda kissed him on the cheek and climbed out of the car. She did the dumb slow walk up to the building again, and again she feared that Jason would never leave. But she fumbled for her keys and he drove away. Brenda sighed and started the long walk to the gas station.

The next morning, Brandon went to the studios of KWBH—a combination sound studio and small office. The studio was barely the size of a walk-in closet, and most of the space was taken up by racks of record albums—old-fashioned vinyl. The Flash was some nerdy-looking kid who did not even remotely match his deep round voice. Brandon had no trouble scoring a little air-time. He just told the Flash, "I'm going to tell all about my date with Marianne Moore."

While a song finished, Brandon went over in his mind the chain of reasoning that had brought him here. He wouldn't take all the blame for what had happened. By sending him flowers, Marianne had thrown the first pebble down a mountainside. But Brandon could not help feeling a little guilty that it was his creative silences, knowing winks, and vague suggestions that had rolled Marianne's innocent pebble into an avalanche of rumor.

The Flash leered at Brandon and opened the mike. Brandon took a deep breath then told him and the listening radio audience that nothing had happened on his date with Marianne.

The Flash blinked and shook his head. He said, "Brandon. The key phrase here is 'Wild Thing.'"

"I know, but listen: All we did was talk."

"You're kidding."

"No. And that may sound a lot less exciting than what you and the rest of the student body had in mind, but it actually meant a lot more."

Evidently, the Flash saw where the interview was going because he lost interest immediately. While he cued up the next record he absentmindedly thanked Brandon for coming in and then pushed him out of the studio. Waiting in the tiny KWBH office was the topic of conversation herself—Marianne.

Brandon was surprised to see her, but glad. He said, "Hi. I guess you heard the big broadcast."

Marianne nodded.

"I've done a lot of stupid stuff lately, but the thing that bums me the most is that you don't think you can trust me anymore. I never meant to hurt you."

"I never meant to let you get so close to me."

Brandon shook his head. "Don't say that. Give me another chance. How about Friday night?"

Marianne kissed him gently on the cheek and whispered into his ear, "I'll call you." A moment later she was gone, leaving Brandon feeling dopey and in love again. Like an idiot, he smiled and waved through the glass at the Flash.

Brenda and Kelly were failing chemistry, and Mr. Ridley had noticed that all their wrong answers were the same. Naturally, he was a dork about it, threatening them both with failure.

Even more frightening, when Brenda told Kelly that she was being forced into a position where she'd have to sleep with Jason, Kelly urged her to admit to him she was only in high school. "If he really loves you, it shouldn't matter. Do you think you love him?"

"I don't know. I think so."

"Then you have to tell him."

She had to tell him. But when? And more important, how?

Brandon knew that because of the misunderstanding over Marianne Moore, his biggest enemy on campus was Andrea Zuckerman. It was important to find Andrea and make sure that she'd heard the KWBH broadcast that morning. He didn't have a chance to talk with her in Spanish class, and the rest of the day raced by without giving him a spare moment.

When school was over, finding Andrea was no problem. Getting her to listen to him was something else. "I never listen to KWBH," she said, "and frankly, I'm not interested in whatever lurid exposé you might have made on the air."

"I didn't—"

But she walked away quickly without letting him finish.

He couldn't leave it there. He couldn't allow Andrea to believe for the rest of her life that he was a total jerk. She'd probably be driving home soon. He'd follow her and force her to listen to him, in her own living room, if necessary.

He ran for Mondale and hoped it would be able to

keep up with whatever dream machine Andrea drove. He slowly rolled the streets around the high school and a few times almost had accidents because he was watching for Andrea instead of paying attention to the traffic.

Then he saw something he found difficult to believe: Andrea Zuckerman standing in line behind a bunch of Hispanic maids, waiting to get on a bus! He had no doubt that it really was Andrea. Just as he pulled up, intending to offer her a ride, she got aboard, and seconds later, the bus pulled away. If Brandon wanted to talk to Andrea, all he could do was follow. She couldn't be going far, right?

Every time the bus stopped, Brandon expected Andrea to get off. She never did. And when the bus roared up onto the northbound San Diego Freeway, he was more astonished and confused than ever.

8

Transformations

TRAFFIC WAS THICKENING. EVEN SO, BRANDON had no trouble following the bus up the freeway. Strange thoughts rolled through his head as he drove. Andrea's car was in the shop. She was going to visit a relative. She was so good at Spanish because the maids helped her with her homework. She was from outer space and going to meet her saucer. Crazy stuff.

Brandon followed the bus through Sepulveda Pass and past the Ventura Freeway interchange. The valley? The valley was the closest you could get to Minneapolis without actually going to Minneapolis. This was truly amazing!

The bus got off at Victory and went east. Soon, it was making stops in middle-class neighborhoods. At one of the stops, Andrea got off. Following a walking person in a car was frustrating, but fortunately,

Brandon did not have to do it for long. Andrea walked up the driveway of a small house. It was neat, clean, well cared for, but it was nothing like the dumps in Beverly Hills. Even the house Brandon lived in was bigger.

He pulled into Andrea's driveway, beeped, waved, and smiled. Andrea whirled on him like a mama bear protecting her young. Bravely, stupidly, Brandon got out of his car and raised his hands in what he hoped was a placating way.

"How dare you follow me!" Andrea cried, "My life is private!" She was so angry, she almost vibrated.

"I just want to talk."

"Sure. You'll go blabbing to everyone about where I live, just like you did about you and Marianne Moore!" Tears had now been added.

Brandon felt bad, but he was well into the situation now. All he could do was try to settle her fears. He asked, "But why do you go *there* if you live *here*?"

"Because West Beverly's the best school in the city, that's why."

"Makes sense to me. But listen: I didn't come here to ruin your life. I want to explain about me and Marianne. That's not who I am. I mean, I'm not perfect, but I'm not a complete jerk either."

Brandon watched Andrea for some sign that she'd understood, some indication that she had actually heard what he'd said. Then he got what he'd been waiting for, a loosening of her posture, a small quirky smile.

She started to explain slowly. "Brandon, All my mail is sent to my grandmother. She lives in Beverly Hills in a cheap rent-controlled apartment." Her voice took on a pleading tone. "If you tell anybody about this, it's going to mess me up really bad. I'll be out of West Beverly High so fast I'll scorch."

Brandon put out his hand and swore, "Your secret is safe with me."

Andrea studied him for a moment, and then she put her hand out to his. They didn't quite shake, but they were friendly. She said, "It's nice to finally bring a friend home from school." Her smile was still quirky, but it was big, warm, and sincere.

Brandon was relieved. He smiled back.

Brenda felt as if she were glowing. Which was probably just as well because despite the very romantic candlelight, Geoffery's Malibu was such a dark restaurant she could barely see her swordfish. Dinner was delicious and Jason was charming. He told her a lot of really private personal stuff and she felt more comfortable with him all the time. If it weren't for what she had to tell him, the evening would have been perfect.

After she'd meditated for a while on the waves, phosphorescing as they curled and crashed, Brenda said, "Jason, do you think I could tell you anything?"

"Of course. Openness is the most important part of a relationship." He had such a beautiful smile.

"You'd still feel the same way no matter what? This could be a shock." God, she sounded as if she were dying of cancer or something. She ought to just tell him.

"Trust me," said Jason. "I'm shockproof." When she continued to hesitate, he frowned with concern and said, "Brenda, what is it?"

Brenda took a deep breath and blurted it out. "I don't live in that sorority house."

"No?"

"No. I don't even go to college."

"You work?"

This was laughable, except that Brenda didn't feel like laughing. She said, "No, Jason. I'm a junior at West Beverly High."

He continued to wait, as if her admission had not registered. At last, he asked, "A junior what?"

"A sixteen-year-old junior."

Jason looked at her with growing alarm, and then everything—his charm, his good looks, everything—was blotted out by his anger. He said, "What is this, some kind of high-school prank? I should sue your parents." He looked around wildly and called for the check.

Seconds later, it seemed, they were out in Jason's car, and Brenda was being driven home. She tried to explain that this relationship had not been easy for her either, that flunking out of school was no fun, that she'd lied to her parents, that he was going to be the first guy she'd ever slept with. His face was grim. He didn't even respond to her till they pulled up in front of her house. Then all he said was, "I'm sorry, Brenda." He tried to put his hand on her arm, but by that time she was so angry and frustrated herself that she shrugged him off and ran from the car.

As Jason's car screeched around the corner her mom came out of the house and took Brenda in her arms. Brenda cried into her shoulder while thinking about what a major idiot she'd been. Her mom tried to calm her by saying it was all right, nothing was that bad, and maybe Mom was right. At the moment, Brenda just wanted to be a high-school kid.

Brenda pulled away a little from her mom and said, "Can we talk about this later? I have a lot of chemistry to catch up on." Her mother smiled understandingly.

Brenda passed her father as she ran into the house. Impulsively, she kissed him on the cheek and kept moving.

On the way up the stairs, she brushed tears from her cheeks and her hand came away black. God, Mom's shoulder must be covered with mascara as well as with tears.

The light was on in Brandon's room and she stopped to look in. "Hi." She said.

Brandon was sprawled on his bed reading. He closed the book on a finger and said, "Hi. What's going on?"

She knew she ought to tell him. He was her brother, her twin. He'd understand. She said, "Brandon, do you mind if I save it for when you're older?"

"I *am* older. A good thirty seconds, at least."

"I know. It's just that when you get to be our age, you know, Brandon, girls are more mature than boys."

"Give me a break," Brandon said, and opened his book again.

Brenda sat down on the bed next to him and said teasingly, "Someday, I'll tell you everything. Almost everything."

Brandon yawned. "I'm already not interested."

Brenda sighed and said, "Nothing was this complicated in Minneapolis."

Brandon looked at her, suddenly very interested. He lowered his voice and asked, "Brenda, did you... ?"

Brenda looked at him sideways and asked, "No. Did you?"

"No."

That seemed to relieve both of them. Brenda was relieved, anyway. She stood up and went to the door. "Brandon, do you think we're going to make it here?"

Brandon shrugged and looked at the floor. "The houses are bigger. The weather is warmer. And the tan lines are outstanding." He looked up and flashed her one of his patented incandescent smiles. "But that doesn't mean they've cracked the meaning of life. You know what I mean?"

Brandon was a great guy. Brenda smiled at him and said, "I know."

As she turned to leave, Brandon called after her, "If you had, would you have told me?"

Brenda laughed as she walked down the hallway to her room to take off the makeup, and magically transform herself back into a high-school kid again.

That night, Brandon dreamed of perfect beaches, of beautiful women in bikinis, and of wild surf. He dreamed of Never-ending Summer. His alarm woke him, and he lay there for a while trying to recapture the ripe languorous mood. It was impossible, so he got up.

Downstairs, Brenda was eating slices of kiwi and marveling at how few calories they had. Their mom was on the phone with Dad. They'd moved all the way from Minneapolis to Beverly Hills, and his first business trip since the move took him to Chicago.

Mrs. Walsh said, "Makes you wonder what we're doing out here, doesn't it?" Brandon could tell she was only half joking. Maybe not even half.

On KWBH, the word for the day was beach. Apparently, Brandon was not the only one who'd been dreaming of sun, sand, and water. When Brenda met Kelly and Donna in the hall, it was the major topic of conversation, right after she introduced them to Brandon.

Kelly said, "I have to work on my back."

"Huh?" Brenda said.

"I spent all last Saturday lying on it, so my tan's totally uneven."

Brenda looked critically at her bare arm. Brandon had to admit that it was pretty pale. Brenda said, "At least you have a *tan*. I look like the Pillsbury Doughboy."

"Start tomorrow," Kelly said excitedly. "Secos Beach. It will be a *major* scene."

Lying in the sun all day sounded like a major bore to Brandon, but he said nothing. Truth was, he had no chance to say anything because Kelly went on about how she was in "desperate need of a new look."

Steve Sanders walked up and said, "With that new nose, you'll need one." He smirked.

If Kelly's looks could kill, Steve would have had three feet of steel poking out his back. He ignored the look and went on, "What's next, Kel? Tummy tuck? Liposuction? Pierced nostril?"

"No, Steve," Kelly said. "I'm just going to have your jaw wired shut."

Brandon took this chance to escape. "Come on, man," he said. "We got class."

Brandon dragged him away, and Steve allowed himself to be dragged, but he was not a happy camper. At the end of the hall, Steve took a last calculating glance back at Kelly and went to English.

Brandon went to the *Blaze* office to see what Andrea had for him. Andrea looked up from proofreading some copy and handed him a piece of paper. "Your next assignment, ace."

Brandon read the few words on the paper and was certain they were for somebody else. He said, "Sorry, I don't do editorials. Especially when they're called," he read from the paper with distaste, "'From the Midwest to West Beverly: A Transfer Student Speaks.' *Boring*!"

"So change the title."

Brandon said nothing. He continued to contemplate Andrea with his eyebrows up.

Andrea shook her head and said, "Just try it, Brandon. You're too good to be only a sports writer."

Very pleased, Brandon asked, "Really? You think?"

"What do *you* think?"

"Okay. I'll try it."

"Great. Due Monday morning. First thing."

As if telling Andrea something she didn't know, Brandon said, "You are relentless."

"I know," Andrea said, and smiled sweetly.

Later, in tech class, Brandon stood behind a blond kid who was young enough to be a freshman, and watched with admiration while he made adjustments to the floor plan on his computer screen. According to the kid, it was the floor plan of the perfect dance club.

"Oh, how sweet."

Brandon looked around and saw the voice had come from an enormous Neolithic guy who may have been a senior for the last five or six years. He and his fat friend had enormous muscles and mean expressions on their faces.

"A little dork with big dreams," the fat friend said.

The freshman had evidently dealt with these two before because he hunkered down and stared fixedly at his screen. He mumbled, "At least I'm not the missing link."

The fat friend grabbed the freshman roughly and said, "What did you say?"

Brandon could see where this ugly scene was

going. Helping the kid would be suicide, but he couldn't see what else to do. Brandon put up a hand and said, "Hey. Take it easy."

The enormous guy leaned over the kid's shoulder and, as if he were trying to figure out fire, said, "Now, where's that 'erase' button?"

9

Surf's up!

"DO US ALL A FAVOR. TOUCH THAT KEYBOARD. Please." It was a voice with the same tone Clint Eastwood used when he invited a punk to make his day.

Four pairs of eyes swung as one to look at the new dude. He was tall and lanky and somehow had a dangerous aura about him. He didn't actually do anything menacing, but something in the way he looked at them, in the way he held his body, told them that menacing was just one possibility.

The fat friend let go of the freshman, and the new dude smiled. He strolled over to stand between the computer and the enormous guy. When he spoke, it was in a quiet dreamy voice that had the hypnotic quality of a growl heard at the back of a dark cave. "Just to be fair, let me tell you something: I'm not in a very good mood today. In fact, I'm feeling sort of, you know, hostile."

"Hey," said the enormous guy, "we didn't mean anything. "We're big fans of the kid's work. Right, Chauncy?"

"You bet, Ralph."

The new dude just smiled. He continued to smile while Chauncy and Ralph rapidly packed up their stuff and left the room. To the freshman, the new dude said, "You're doing a fine job, kid. Keep up the good work." The menace was gone from his voice, but it was still tough.

The new dude moseyed out the door after Chauncy and Ralph.

"Who was that masked man?" Brandon asked.

Like Brandon, the freshman was wide-eyed with wonder. "I never saw the guy before in my life."

Brandon was too curious to let a guy like that pass unquestioned. He hurried after him and found him at his locker. He put out his hand and said, "I'm Brandon Walsh."

"Brandon Walsh," the dude repeated, then asked, "Scotch or Irish?"

"Both. By way of Minnesota."

"Dylan McKay," the dude said. He took Brandon's hand firmly and shook it.

Brandon said, "That was great, what you did to those two nimrods."

Dylan shrugged as if he were being complimented on holding open a door for an old lady. "I don't believe in winning through intimidation unless I'm doing the intimidating."

Dylan didn't say any more. He looked perfectly comfortable lounging against his locker. But Brandon felt as if the conversation were dying, and with it a possible friendship. He said, "You hungry? I have next period free. We could grab a little fuel—"

"Sure," Dylan said sarcastically. "Let's do lunch."

I shouldn't have said that, Brandon thought. Must I speak in clichés? Worse yet, in Beverly Hills clichés?

Perhaps noticing Brandon's discomfort, Dylan suddenly said, "Don't see much water in Minnesota."

"Lakes. No oceans."

"My sympathies." He snapped his fingers and came to attention. "Come on."

"Where are we going?" Brandon said as he strode after Dylan.

"Field trip," Dylan said cryptically.

Dylan led Brandon to his cherry Porsche and drove him away with the wind in his hair. Brandon tried to feel guilty—the school day was not over and he had that editorial to write. As a matter of fact, Brandon tried to tell Dylan about the editorial, but Dylan seemed unimpressed. When they got where they were going, Brandon saw why.

They stepped out onto the beach of his dreams: blue sky, creaming surf, golden sand. The air had a gentle touch that was warm and salty. Everything was so beautiful, it all really took Brandon's breath away. Very few people were around, which made the place seem even more magical.

A couple of guys in wet suits were sitting on surfboards in the water, riding up and down on the swell. One called to Dylan, "Yo, McKay!" The other one cried, "Get in the green room!" Nearby, on a board of her own, was a girl who said nothing.

Great, thought Brandon. I'll have to learn another language.

Dylan introduced Brandon to the three on the surfboards, Duane, Eric, and Betty. Duane and Eric were nearly interchangeable. Duane was a little taller, and the obvious leader, but they were both big blond surfer guys, complete with rad rags and unbelievable tans. They were even good surfers. Betty was pretty, with the regulation blond hair. But she seemed a little waif-like and distracted.

Dylan got Brandon into a pair of baggies and attached his ankle with a rubber cord to a boogie board, which was a very short surfboard that is generally ridden lying on your stomach. The ocean was a big powerful beast, the likes of which Brandon had never tangled with before. He swam out, waited for a wave, and tried to ride it in. The wave threw him into the air, and when he came down, he swallowed salt water. His ears were full of water, too, but he could hear Dylan call "Wipeout!" and either Duane or Eric cry, "Hoe-dad! Grem-mie!"

Brandon felt for the bottom with his feet, and shaking water from his ears and sputtering, he crawled up onto the beach.

From somewhere, Dylan called, "Yo, Minnesota! You okay?"

Was he okay? Okay? Brandon stood up, waved his fists in the air, and bellowed, "I love this!"

He had never felt so alive in his life.

But surfing, even just boogie boarding, was surprisingly tiring. Playing cat-and-mouse with the ocean was not easy work. Brandon found that muscles he hadn't even known he had were now sore. So he sat on the beach with Betty. She told him that the green room was not just the ocean, but the gnarliest place in it. "When you're inside the green room, you're riding the perfect wave."

"Very heavy," Brandon said. After watching the

three guys paddle out to a spot where they could wait for the next wave, he said, "You go to West Beverly?"

Betty laughed and said, "Are you kidding? I live in the valley. The deepest, darkest valley." From her tone, Brandon decided she didn't think much of the place.

"How do you know Dylan?"

Betty shrugged. "I don't. I mean, who does? I mean, the dude is not exactly an open book." She shrugged again. "Not that he'd let me read him anyway." She'd been watching the ocean. Now she looked down at the sand.

Brandon was not one to make snap judgments about people, but he'd been watching Betty and the two surf gods interact since he arrived, and he was pretty sure that Betty was one very sorry chick. She had everything it took to be a big social success, everything except the faith that she had anything at all. She let Duane and Eric push her around.

Hoping to get her talking again, Brandon asked, "If Dylan's not exactly your best bro, what's he doing here?"

"He just hangs with us to bust a few with Duane and Eric." She watched to see how Brandon reacted when she said, "My real name's Sarah. Duane and Eric call me 'Betty' because that's what they think I am— just some betty, a dumb surf bunny." She pointed to her surfboard, and with more pride than Brandon would have expected, she said, "But I have a stick of my own, and I can match any guy on it."

Brandon smiled at her and said, "I bet you can."

For the first time, Sarah smiled. She was generally *Sarah* when she smiled. Brandon thought that even at this early stage, he could tell when she was in Sarah Mode and when she was in Betty Mode.

"You're really nice," Sarah said.

Brandon shrugged. "I'm from out of town."

"I can tell." She then told him that they were on the beach every morning at six. "Sunrise surf. It's awesome."

It sounded like an invitation to Brandon. He grabbed at it. "I'm there, Sarah."

She looked at him up from under, shyly.

The day was long and tiring, but it was a tired that Brandon enjoyed. It loosened him down instead of tightening him up.

His mom was whistling when he got home. She was surrounded by bubbling pots, bowls of ingredients, swirls of good-smelling steam. "Welcome-home dinner," she explained. "Your father *will* return this evening."

But around five, she got a call from him to say that he had to stay another night in Chicago. Brandon could see that she was trying to make light of it when his mom said, "Well, so much for the big welcomeback feast." She waved her eyebrows at Brandon and said, "Which means there'll be more for the three of us."

Brandon wasn't fooled. He could guess how disappointed she must be. Which was why it was even harder than it might have been for him to say, "Make that two. The paper assigned me an editorial."

Brandon saw that his mom was surprised to hear that, and more than a little disappointed at losing another family member to outside life. But she smiled bravely and veered off into the new subject. She said, "Very impressive. About what?"

"Oh, about what it's like to move here from Minneapolis. I figure I'm good for a few more hours at the library before my brain crashes and burns." Even as he moved toward the kitchen door, he wondered if he was doing the right thing. He had to say no when his mom offered him a sandwich or something to keep him going. He got out the door just before he was actually lured into staying.

Dylan was waiting for him a few houses down. As they sped away, Dylan asked, "Did we get Daddy's permission?"

What the hell, Brandon thought. He said, "No, we got Mom's." He met Dylan's grin with a grin of his own.

10

Hip hopping

BRENDA HELD A PAIR OF HER GOOD JEANS against her body as she looked at herself in the mirror. They would do. Part of her—the Minnesota part, probably—thought that creatively ripping the knees on a perfectly good pair of pants was a bad idea. But perfect jeans were out this year, and she certainly couldn't afford one of those preripped pairs Kelly had bought that afternoon.

Brenda sighed dramatically. Being poor was a drag, she thought. Okay, they weren't *really* poor. They didn't live in a doorway or anything; on the other hand, nobody in her family could go into a store and just buy anything they wanted without thinking about it. That afternoon, Brenda had seen Kelly charge almost a thousand bucks' worth of clothes in one store without hesitation. Even a thing like poverty was sometimes relative.

Brenda had the scissors in her hand, ready to do the deed, when her mom came in and offered to help. Mom was a great seamstress and sometimes even made her own clothes. "I need all the help I can get," Brenda said.

While they ripped out seams, artistically slashed the legs, and sewed on colorful patches, Mrs. Walsh said, "That school paper certainly keeps your brother busy."

That sounded like a trick statement to Brenda, designed to elicit information. Carefully, she said, "I'm swamped enough with just normal schoolwork."

As she hand-sewed an American-flag patch, Mrs. Walsh said, "More homework. Bigger houses. Better clothes."

"Not better," Brenda said firmly, "just more expensive."

"I'm glad you know the difference."

"Knowing the difference doesn't mean I enjoy watching Kelly give her credit cards a workout."

Brenda and her mom thought about that, about what it would be like to just take everything for granted. Would it be fun after the novelty wore off? Brenda knew she'd like to find out. She was pretty sure she'd never get the chance.

Dylan told him that only tourists called the street the Sunset Strip, but Brandon had trouble thinking of it any other way. Bright cars moved along it in a steady stream in both directions, almost blocking intersections at red lights. There was a constant whoosh and the occasional blast of a car horn. Even the billboards had more flash and dash than the billboards in other parts of town. They had moving parts, smoke, glitter, three-dimensional attachments, and they were mostly for new CDs and movies.

Office buildings stood wall to wall with comedy clubs, music clubs, small theaters, fancy restaurants, high-powered delicatessens. The people who walked the narrow sidewalks came in all sizes, styles, and types.

Some were obviously street people, their hair strung out and dirty, their clothes picked from some rag bin, their shoes worn or nonexistent. Very fresh kids of all ages were obviously parading their most outrageous clothes—Brandon assumed they were the *most* outrageous—a very hip hodgepodge of tights, ripped jeans, skimpy or colorful tops, shoes with more buckles than they seemed to need. Self-mutilation was very big. Even guys wore earrings, of course, but some of these kids had six or eight in one ear, and more than a few had rings in their noses.

Very cool, Brandon and Dylan leaned against the Porsche, watching the passing parade. Brandon was impressed that Dylan had actually found a place to park.

By accident or design, Duane, Eric, and Betty found them. They wore Maui and Sons T-shirts and baggie jams with grotesque Hawaiian patterns on them. Dylan was not very enthusiastic when Duane and Eric wanted to join forces, but he invited Betty along. For a moment, Brandon thought Betty might come away with them, but her nerve failed her, and she stuck with Duane and Eric. Very softly she whispered, "We'll follow you."

When Brandon got back into the car next to Dylan, he was surprised to find a book of poems by Lord

Byron tucked between the front seats. Dylan tried to laugh it off, saying that like Lord Byron, he was "mad, bad, and dangerous to know," but Brandon thought that might be a cover for a sincere interest in poetry. He was certain Dylan was more than just a cool personality with two legs.

They drove up the strip to a fancy hotel called the Bel Age; it was a tower of wood, brass, and colored light in the center of everything. Dylan left his Porsche with a uniformed valet and encouraged Duane to do the same with his Jeep.

Inside, the cool conditioned air spoke of old money in new bills. Brandon was aware that he gaped as they crossed the lobby of white marble. He wasn't dressed right for this place. None of them was. What were they doing here? Following Dylan, that was what.

The polished brass doors of the elevator opened, and Dylan took them to the third floor, where he walked down the maroon carpet, trying doorknobs. Brandon's feeling of dread grew stronger with every step. Dylan found an unlocked door and threw it open. With a ta-dah! motion, he stepped inside and invited the others to enter. Beyond, was a room tastefully furnished in brownish tones not often seen outside a display of lady's stockings. Brandon knew that whatever was going on wasn't for him.

Duane and Eric were very excited. Even Betty let Brandon down by exclaiming, "This is so outrageous!"

Brandon stood at the threshold and said, "Come on, Dylan. Let's get out of here and grab a burger."

Dylan smiled devilishly and said, "I have a better idea. Let's stay here and have a burger." He picked up the phone and actually had the industrial-strength nerve to call room service!

When Brandon said he was history, Betty encouraged him to stay and he almost did. But ultimately, he couldn't see waiting around to get busted for breaking and entering.

Brandon had actually made it as far as the lobby when Dylan bounded out of the emergency stairwell and caught him by the arm. Brandon was about to shake him off when a waiter dressed in tails wheeled up a silver tray carrying burgers and fries and respectfully said to Dylan, "Excuse me, Mr. McKay. Will you and your friends be eating on the terrace or up in your suite?"

"Upstairs is cool, Tony," Dylan said as if he'd said things like it a thousand times before.

Tony bowed and pushed his silver tray toward the bank of elevators, leaving Brandon confused and gaping even more widely than he had before. "You live here?" he asked, incredulous.

"I do. In Dad's corporate pad. It's mine when he's out of town, which is mostly." He shook his head, more in pity than in anger, and went on, "My parents are not exactly into parenting."

Brandon wasn't sure which was worse, committing a crime, or pretending to commit a crime in order to impress somebody. Either way, he was disgusted.

Dylan stopped him from walking away when he said, "Come on, Brandon, stick around. Ol' Henry downstairs makes the best fries in town." He smiled in a conspiratorial way. "But don't tell 'em upstairs. We wouldn't want to spoil the fun. *And* ruin my reputation."

Brandon shook his head and, with some venom, said, "You're right. I wouldn't want to ruin the only thing you care about."

Without waiting for Dylan to say anything more, Brandon walked quickly from the lobby and out into the Sunset Strip night, a night that had gone rancid.

The next morning was Saturday, and Brandon suffered through the usual bathroom traffic jam with Brenda. When he got inside, he saw that she was wearing tastefully ripped jeans and a sherbet-colored bikini top and was just finishing doing whatever girls do for hours in the bathroom.

While he brushed his teeth, he admitted that he hadn't been studying the night before, but had been on the Sunset Strip ("or whatever it's cool to call it") and then at the Bel Age Hotel with a guy named Dylan McKay.

When Brenda heard about this, Brandon could see that she was already calculating ways to get to know Dylan McKay better. He said, "No way, Bren."

Brenda surprised him by saying, "No way is right. Everybody knows that guy is major trouble." Excited by the exotic nature of the crime, she went on, "I heard he got this girl in Paris pregnant."

"I wouldn't be surprised."

Further discussion was stopped by a horn honking outside. With his mouth still full of toothpaste, Brandon looked out the window and saw Kelly Taylor, dressed approximately the same way as Brenda, but with a smaller top and more rips in her pants.

"I bet she looks great," Brenda said, not even getting close to the window.

"She looks like some kind of fashion victim. *You* look great."

"Thanks, Brandon." On her way out of the bathroom, she called, "Come on if you're coming."

"I'm still not happy with that editorial."

Brenda stopped and looked back at him. "You're not happy, period. I mean, all you do is study."

He wasn't happy with the editorial because he hadn't really started it yet. But it would be so easy to give in. The sun. The sand. The girls. Brandon was only human. Maybe if he rested his brain, something would come to him. He would write the editorial tomorrow.

Brandon sat in the backseat with Brenda, which was a little embarrassing, but he kept telling himself that nobody outside the car would know she was his sister.

As it turned out, the closer they got to the beach, the more Brandon knew that he, that all of them, had made a mistake. None of them spoke of it, not even while Kelly carefully negotiated her red BMW through the crowded parking lot looking for a space. But the sun could not get through the lowering gray clouds. A cool—all right, cold—wind blew across the sand.

Even so, the beach was crowded with kids throwing Frisbees, playing volleyball and smash ball. Many of them were in bare feet, but otherwise wore jeans and sweatshirts. Each group had its own music that came from a radio or tape player.

Brandon followed the girls down to the water, kicking up sand like Lawrence of Arabia. He was glad his mom had forced him to take a lumberjack shirt, "just in case it gets chilly." Brenda wore her University of Minnesota sweatshirt, Donna had thrown on a coat that was much too fancy for the gig, but Kelly had nothing on except her very hip and expensive outfit. She was definitely turning blue in the cold. "Worse yet," she said, "I don't see a single person I want to talk to."

As if on cue, Steve walked up to them and, very pleased with the situation, said, "Hi, Kel. Warm enough for you?" As usual, Steve was much too hip for the scene, but at least his leather jacket must have been keeping him from freezing. The Beachboys baseball cap was a nice touch.

"Just cool," Kelly said angrily. "As in most hip."

Steve laughed and pulled Brandon aside as the girls walked on, in search of the perfect spot to deposit their towels, radios, magazines, and various lotions.

Steve glanced around to make sure nobody important was listening and said, "Have you seen David Silver?"

Brandon was amazed. David Silver was a mere freshman and the guy who was reponsible for the previously crunched condition of Steve's Corvette. He said, "The David Silver who goes to West Beverly High? That David Silver?"

"Yeah. His dad is a TV producer and my mom wants to be on his new show. She thinks being nice to David will help her get the part."

"I guess being nice to him won't do permanent damage to either of you."

"Unless somebody sees us together. Just tell him I'm looking for him, okay?"

"No problem."

Steve walked off, continuing his search for David Silver. Brandon knew that Steve couldn't be happy spending his afternoon looking for a *guy*, and a *freshman* at that.

Steve was gone. Brandon's sister and her friends had evaporated. He was alone. But that was okay. It gave him the chance to look for something, too. He wanted to find the green room.

11

The beach is *so* cool

BEYOND THE FRINGES OF THE WEST BEVERLY party, a tax bracket, a 'tude, and a dream session away, Brandon found them. But they weren't surfing. They were sharing a tall brown bottle. Betty found everything Brandon said to be hilarious, but whatever was in the bottle just made Duane and Eric surly. They were very possessive about this stretch of beach and made big noises about clobbering any West Beverly kid who came their way. Luckily for Brandon, in their present condition, they never connected him with the enemy.

Soon Duane and Eric got tired of hurling clever remarks at Brandon's disapproving face. They handed the brown bottle to Betty and went reeling down the beach, holding each other up, and sort of singing an old Jan and Dean hit.

Betty thrust the bottle at Brandon and offered him

a drink. Brandon declined. She giggled at him. Brandon just shook his head and said, "See you later."

"Hey, wait," Betty called after him. "I was just being friendly."

Brandon waited for her to catch up, then turned to face her. "You were friendlier yesterday. You were also a sober girl named Sarah."

The girl—at the moment she was Betty—tried to put her arms around Brandon's neck, but he backed away. "I thought you liked me," she said.

"I like a girl named Sarah. This isn't her."

Brandon walked away. Behind him, he heard Betty—definitely Betty—giggle again and shout, "More for me."

Brandon felt really bad about leaving her like that. But to drink or not to drink was her choice. He would have helped her if she'd asked for it, but she seemed determined to let herself be used, and to hang around with those two bozos.

He walked back toward the West Beverly party thinking about life, thinking about school, thinking about the editorial he had yet to write, when somebody yelled, "Yo, Minnesota," from the water. Brandon stopped and watched Dylan march out of the ocean with a surfboard under his arm.

Dylan dropped his board at Brandon's feet and said, "Last night was supposed to be fun, you know. If it wasn't, well, I apologize."

"It wasn't, and I accept your apology." They shook on it, then looked way up the beach to where Duane and Eric teased Betty by tossing the brown bottle up and back between them. Brandon said, "I don't understand why you hang with those two dorks."

"I don't hang with them. At the moment, I am

hanging with you. I'm doing it because I'm sorry about last night and I want to be your friend."

"You already apologized. I'm cool."

"Great." Dylan hefted his board and said, "You coming?"

Brandon was tempted. He'd never met anyone like Dylan before and he was fascinated. But there would be other times. He said, "I have to find my sister."

Dylan nodded and said, "I'm outta here." He turned away, but Brandon stopped him by saying, "I heard a rumor about you and a girl in Paris."

Dylan turned around, smiling with secret knowledge. He said, "Don't believe it." He waited a beat. "The girl was in Argentina." He walked away, leaving Brandon not knowing what to believe. Evidently, Dylan enjoyed being a man of mystery. Brandon wondered if someday it would all get a little old.

By the time Brandon returned to the zone where the West Beverly beach party was happening, a lot of the kids had given up waiting for the sun and gone home. Being surrounded by empty sand, Brenda and her friends were easy to spot.

He passed Steve talking to David Silver. David seemed stunned by the sudden attention bestowed upon him. He smiled and nodded and didn't say much. As Brandon passed, Steve rolled his eyes at him. Talking to a freshman in public. A grotty deal for sure.

Even wearing her sweatshirt, Brenda was cold. She was lonely, too, but the sweatshirt could not be expected to help with that. Donna tried to be agreeable, but it was clear that she also thought the current subarctic beach scene was pretty bogus. Despite her goose bumps, Kelly seemed determined to pretend she was enjoying herself. And then they were almost alone on the beach and even pretending no longer seemed reasonable.

Suddenly, Kelly stood up and announced that she was leaving. She and Donna began to collect their stuff. Brenda said, "I'll go find Brandon." Coming toward them was a lone figure who looked like a good prospect. Brenda ran to meet him.

She passed Steve Sanders, who for some reason was talking to a freshman, of all things. Steve was smiling, but he didn't look happy.

The closer she got to the lone figure, the more certain Brenda was that it was Brandon. They met and assured each other that the time to leave had come.

"I guess so," said Brandon. "There goes Kelly."

Brenda whirled and watched in disbelief as Donna and Kelly rode out of the parking lot in the unmistakable red BMW.

"I don't believe this," Brenda said. So much for friendship, she thought. So much for loyalty.

"I can," Brandon said in a way that Brenda thought was needlessly nasty. "Come on. Someone'll give us a lift."

She and Brandon collected her stuff, which was sitting unprotected on the beach, and began to walk in the direction Brandon had indicated. Brenda looked out at the crashing gray ocean and said, "It's amazing that people will surf in this cold."

Brandon glanced out at the water, then seemed to see something that she had missed, because he suddenly threw her stuff at her and ran off. Brenda called after him, but he was already yards down the beach, and the wind whirled her voice away.

He stopped only to pull off his shoes, and then he dived into the cold water and began to swim. Brenda could see now what he was making for. It was a figure lying down on a surfboard, just at the shore break. Before he got to her, though, the figure slipped into the water and Brandon cried, "Sarah!"

Brenda ran to the tide line and fretfully scanned the water. "There, Brandon," she cried, and pointed at the spot where the figure had momentarily surfaced. Brandon swam out to her and dived. For a moment, Brenda thought he'd drowned, then he surfaced and swam with the figure until his feet touched bottom; he carried the surfer onto the dry sand.

The figure was a girl who must have been pretty under other circumstances. At the moment, water ran from her mouth, and under the tan her skin looked a little blue.

Brandon leaned over to blow into her lungs. He stopped just long enough to yell, "Nine-one-one, Brenda! Now!"

Brenda ran for a public phone.

12

The green room

BRENDA PRAYED SHE WOULD FIND A PHONE ON the side of the bathhouse and she did. She called 911, explained the nature of the emergency, and in what seemed like seconds, an ambulance arrived.

Not long after that, Brenda and Brandon were sitting wrapped in dry towels in a Malibu hospital emergency room. They were both a little dazed by the speed at which things had happend, but Brenda looked at Brandon with new eyes. She had never personally seen anyone do anything so brave. She had no doubt that he was a hero.

The doctor said that the girl—whose name turned out to be Sarah or Betty, Brenda was never clear on which—was probably an alcoholic, because of the temperature of her body and the alcohol in her system. She needed a little rest, but would be okay. Brandon just shook his head.

When their mom showed up to take her and
Brandon home, the doctor called them *both* heroes.
Brenda liked the sound of that, and Brandon seemed
willing to go for it, but she felt that her part in the affair
had been rather small.

All the way home Mom talked about how life in
Beverly Hills differed from life in Minneapolis. She
saw this escapade at the beach as part of the same pat-
tern that contained her husband's extended stay in
Chicago. She said, "If this is a day in the life of your
basic Beverly Hills family, we're moving back to
Minnesota."

Brenda and Brandon traded glances. Was Mom
serious? Or was that just her concern talking? Brenda
thought perhaps this was not a good time to ask.
They'd find out eventually anyway.

Brandon had never been so tired in his life. Still,
he could not sleep; something kept nagging at him.
He must have slept a little after all, because when he
looked at the clock again, it read five-twelve.

Sarah's statement, "Sunrise surf. It's awesome,"
kept playing in his head. It kept him company as he
dressed in the dark and then hurried downstairs. It
would not leave him alone.

Beverly Hills at sunrise was a beautiful place. The
air was cool and cleaner than it had been at sunset.
Shadows lightened into unbelievably pure colors. The
only company he had on the road were garbage trucks,
and then, very early commuters. They were all part of
the early-morning brotherhood.

"Sunrise surf. . ."

Driving across town was a breeze and a pleasure,

but Secos Beach was far away, and it was nearly six by the time Brandon got there. He drove across the empty parking lot till he was parallel with three guys standing by their boards scoping the waves. It was Duane, Eric, and Dylan, of course.

When they saw him, Duane waved and said, "Hey, dude."

Duane was a heydude. Brandon hated guys like that.

Dylan barely glanced in his direction and said, "Minnesota! Glad you could make it."

Eric said, "Where's your stick, dude?"

His stick. His surfboard. He didn't need one. He hadn't come here to surf.

Brandon shook his head. His voice was unsteady when he said, "You think that because you surf you're cool. But I'll tell you something. You're not cool. You're scum."

"Excuse me?" Eric said, his voice sharp.

"No way. Not now. Not ever."

Dylan put up a hand and said, "Whoa there, Brandon—"

Dylan was interrupted by Eric throwing a punch at Brandon. Brandon ducked and tackled him around the waist and they both went down in the sand, scuffling around. Duane grabbed Brandon from behind and held his arms while Eric paid him back for the bloody lip Brandon had given him. Again and again, Eric punched Brandon hard in the stomach, until Dylan shoved Brandon one way and the two surfers the other. They lay in the sand gasping. Brandon had a dull throbbing pain in his gut.

Dylan touched Brandon's leg with his toe and asked, "What happened to her?"

Brandon took a shallow ragged breath and said, "Call Malibu Hospital. They'll tell you."

"Hey, we didn't know," Duane said.

Brandon said, "You didn't *care* either." He stood up, swatted sand from his hands, and walked away, so angry that he hoped Duane and Eric would jump him again. He gently touched his stomach where it hurt.

Somebody put a hand on his arm, and Brandon turned with his fist ready. Then he saw it was Dylan. Dylan put up his hands and smiled. They walked along the beach together.

"Thanks," Brandon said. He grimaced at the pain and tried to walk in a different way.

Dylan shrugged and said, "More nimrods."

"Yeah."

"You up for breakfast?"

Brandon thought over Dylan's question. Once more, he was tempted. But he was also eager to get home. He knew what to write about in his editorial. He decided to broach a different subject. He said, "You don't let people in, do you?"

"Not if I can help it." Dylan smiled again. "Of course, sometimes I make an exception."

Brandon thought he knew what Dylan meant, and he felt good about it. They parted at Brandon's car after agreeing to have that breakfast sometime soon.

By the time he got home, the pain in Brandon's stomach was no more than a warm ache, as if he'd eaten too much pizza. Other things had also improved. Not only had he thought of a way to approach his editorial, but while he'd been at the beach, his mom had received a call that Dad had made *from the plane*. He would absolutely be home in a few hours. Of course, Brenda was still not speaking to Kelly, but Brandon couldn't decide if that was a good thing or a bad thing.

He spent a lot of time in his room banging at his computer. After a while, the editorial began to take shape. He kept working until he had the editorial as perfect as he could make it. He read it over one more time:

There's an expression surfers use for the curl of a perfect wave. It's called "the green room," and getting inside it is the peak of the ride.

To a new student like me, "the green room" might as well be West Beverly High School, because getting inside it—into the "in" crowd, the "in" parties, the "in" clothes, and the "in" cars— requires a skill they never taught us back in Minnesota. That was what I thought when I took "the green room" at face value, when I believed people's images and played along with them.

I know better now. I've learned that appearances can be very deceiving, and if you believe them, you deceive yourself more than anyone else. So when you meet me in the halls, or in class, or on the lawn at lunch, I'll be looking for more than meets the eye. And I hope you will, too. Because *inside* is where "the green room" really is.

Brandon had to admit it wasn't bad, but he still had to try it out on his harshest critic. He took it to Brenda. She looked at the typed pages as if they were dead frogs. "What is it?" she said.

"Just read," Brandon said, and pressed the pages at her.

She took it with the resignation that only a sister can show when doing a favor for a brother. Brandon went to stand in the doorway and tried not to watch her. But he saw her glance at him a few times. When she finished, she let the pages lie in her lap and said, "Brandon, that's beautiful."

"You think?"

Brenda sighed and said, "I'm so touched I may even call Kelly and forgive her."

"Don't do anything hasty."

Brandon thanked Brenda for reading the editorial, and Brenda thanked him for *letting* her read the editorial. As he was about to leave, Brenda said, "Just remember me when they all want to get into *your* 'green room.'"

On Monday morning, Brandon and Brenda had trouble getting through the halls without being congratulated, slapped on the back, given the high-five, and generally mobbed in a good-natured way. Word was out that they'd saved somebody's life over the weekend. They slunk around, calling as little attention to themselves as they could.

Brandon was on his way to the *Blaze* office when Steve took up a position alongside him. As they walked through the crowded halls, Steve shook his head in disgust.

"What?" asked Brandon.

"You know David Silver's father?"

"Not personally, but—"

"He's the wrong Mel Silver."

"Wrong?"

"Mel Silver. My mom wanted me to make friends with the son of Mel Silver, the TV producer. David Silver's father is some kind of dentist."

"Tough," said Brandon. Could anybody really take this stuff seriously? "Gotta go," he said, and dived into the *Blaze* office.

He turned in his editorial right on time and Andrea loved it. "Glad I let you talk me into writing it," Brandon said. As he left the *Blaze* office, he ran into Sarah. Definitely Sarah. Not Betty. Brandon was surprised but pleased.

Sarah told him she was all right. "Clean bill of health, at least physically. My parents want me to join a program."

"That's a good idea," said Brandon, feeling a little like a parent himself.

Sarah stepped closer to Brandon and put a hand on his shoulder. She said, "I guess you can figure out what my feelings are about you, about what you did. . . ." She let her voice trail off suggestively.

Brandon hugged her and whispered into her ear, "My last name's Walsh. We're listed."

"That should be easy," she whispered back. "You're probably the only ones who are."

Brandon watched her walk away. She waved and rounded a corner. A moment later, Brenda walked up with Kelly. Something was definitely different about them. Then Brandon knew what it was. Kelly was trying to keep up with Brenda instead of vice versa. This was very interesting.

Brenda said, "I see that girl is okay."

"Yeah," said Brandon. "I think she has her life wired at last."

Kelly waited for an opening and then said, "See you at lunch, Brenda?"

Brenda thought over Kelly's question. Whether she was really considering or just playing the moment for its drama, Brandon couldn't tell.

At last, Brenda said, "Sure."

"Great," Kelly said, and squeezed Brenda's hand before she walked away.

Brandon said, "Know what? I think we're going to make it here."

"Speak for yourself."

Evidently, Brenda was not as confident as she had led Kelly to believe. Brandon decided to twist the knife a little. He said, "I was."

"Oh, you!" Brenda said, and punched him in the shoulder.

13

The domino theory

THE WEEK WAS QUIET UNTIL BRENDA HEARD
about the twilight horseback ride that was to take place
on an impending Friday night. Just everybody was
going, but her parents didn't understand. They said it
cost too much. And they reminded her constantly that
she had never ridden a horse. She decided to stress
her desire for new experiences.

It was now early Thursday morning. Brenda was
outside, helping her mother with the gardening till
Brandon came downstairs *at last*. She handed her
mom the stuff she needed: watering can; shovel; plant.
Her mother still wasn't buying the new-experiences
argument. And the ride was still too expensive.

"I'm nobody here," Brenda said dejectedly. "I have
no clothes—"

While she built a little mound of dirt to support the

stem of a dahlia, Mrs. Walsh said, "Seems to me what you're wearing fits all the definitions of clothes."

Brenda was not convinced. Covering one's body was not enough.

Mrs. Walsh glanced sideways at Brenda and said, "Look, Brenda, if people think well of you only for your appearance, they don't really think well of *you*."

A typical Mom argument. They weren't getting anywhere. Brandon bounded out of the house, collected her, and they headed out for school in Mondale. What a drag.

While Mrs. Walsh continued to plant her flowers a short leathery brown-skinned woman approached. She wore jeans and a plaid shirt. The jeans were not fashionable, but they looked as if they would wear like iron. The woman spoke to Mrs. Walsh in Spanish, which Mrs. Walsh didn't understand.

Eventually it became clear that the woman's name was Anna, and that she intended to clean the Walsh's house. When Mrs. Walsh went inside to call her husband about this, Anna somehow came, too. She began cleaning even as Mrs. Walsh dialed the phone. Mrs. Walsh watched her nervously.

Mrs. Walsh explained the situation, and after a moment, Mr. Walsh said, "Hey, I know who she is. Alan's wife mentioned that her cleaning lady had a cousin who needed work."

"Thanks for asking my opinion."

"It completely slipped my mind." Behind Mr. Walsh, Mrs. Walsh could hear phones ringing and people talking. Mr. Walsh went on hurriedly, "I thought you'd like it. Everyone in Beverly Hills has a maid."

"You sound like Brenda."

"Come on, honey, you had someone in Minneapolis."

"Only a few hours a week. And I also had friends, a life, a world—"

Suddenly Mr. Walsh was gone, and at the other end of the line was only a busy signal. "—a phone that worked," Mrs. Walsh grumbled as she hung up.

Anna was scrubbing the kitchen sink. Mrs. Walsh smiled at her in a weak and uncertain way.

As she got her books Brenda saw Tiffany Morgan and Kelly laughing together. Kelly looked at herself in the mirror inside her locker while trying on something that looked like a pirate hat.

Whereas Kelly looked like a very cute high-school girl, Tiffany Morgan looked like some kind of high-fashion model, with the cheekbones and the clothes to go with it. The pirate hat was obviously hers.

Brenda sidled up to Donna, who was also watching this display, and said, "I didn't know Tiffany and Kelly were such good friends."

"*Ex* such good friends," Donna said. She lowered her voice and said meaningfully, "From grade school."

Brenda could understand that. The grade-school friends you actually kept were yours forever.

The hat had come from Nitro, the newest, hottest, most awesome boutique going at that moment. Kelly, Tiffany, and Donna conspired to go there after school. Brenda was feeling a little left out when Tiffany suddenly turned to her and asked, "Want to come?"

Brenda quickly ran over her available cash. She could just about manage a cheeseburger, no fries. She said, "I can't." She shrugged and giggled. "My American Express card—I left home without it."

"No money necessary," said Tiffany. "Just fun."

Brenda nodded enthusiastically.

While Kelly and Tiffany giggled the day away Brenda hung around the fringes. She felt lost and betrayed by Kelly, though Tiffany sometimes tried to drag her into the conversation. Brenda answered and she existed for a moment, and then she was the little girl who wasn't there again.

In English class, Ms. Rye talked about *Les Misérables* by Victor Hugo. Ms. Rye was beautiful *and* smart. She worked her students pretty hard, but she was a good teacher, and just about everybody liked her. Brenda thought some of the guys might be in love with her.

Les Misérables was about this guy named Jean Valjean, who had to steal bread to feed his family. For this, the French police put him into a terrible prison for twenty years. Twenty years! Brenda found the whole situation fascinating, like watching a line of standing dominoes. Knock the first one over and they all fell over. Could she steal under those circumstances, or would she rather die? She couldn't decide.

When Ms. Rye asked Tiffany what *she* thought of Jean Valjean's crime, Tiffany said, "'Let them eat cake!'" which got a laugh out of everybody, including Ms. Rye. It was Friday afternoon, after all. As the bell rang to end the school day Ms. Rye reminded them about the paper that was due on Monday. "Remember, explore how one's whole life can be changed by one decision, by one event."

As she and Kelly and Donna walked out of the room Tiffany said, "What will change my life right now

Jason Priestley as Brandon Walsh. *Photo credit: Andrew Semel*

Shannen Doherty as Brenda Walsh.
Photo credit: Timothy White

Luke Perry as Dylan McKay. *Photo credit: Timothy White*

Jennie Garth
as Kelly Taylor.
Photo credit:
E.J. Camp

Tori Spelling as Donna Martin. *Photo credit: Andrew Semel*

The boys of West Beverly High. Jason Priestley, Ian Ziering, and Luke Perry. *Photo credit: Timothy White*

Surf's up for the Beverly Hills, 90210 beach patrol. *From left to right:* Luke Perry, Brian Austin Green, Ian Ziering, and Jason Priestley. *Photo credit: Andrew Semel*

Checking out the beach scene with the girls from West Beverly High. *From left to right:* Jennie Garth, Shannen Doherty, and Tori Spelling. *Photo credit: Andrew Semel*

Fun in the sun for the cast of Beverly Hills, 90210. *From left to right:* Tori Spelling, Brian Austin Green, Gabrielle Carteris, Jason Priestley, Shannen Doherty, Luke Perry, Jennie Garth and Ian Ziering. *Photo credit: Andrew Semel*

The bathing beauties of West Beverly High. From left to right: Tori Spelling, Shannen Doherty, and Jennie Garth. *Photo credit: Andrew Semel*

"Welcome to the Green Room." Brandon contemplates the surf scene with Dylan for the first time.
Photo: ©1991 Torand, a Spelling Ent. Co.

Luke Perry as the coolest guy at West Beverly high, Dylan McKay. *Photo credit: Andrew Semel*

is a little heavy-duty shopping at Nitro."

Just to remind them she was there, Brenda agreed.

Brandon had taken names and addresses from the JOBS bulletin board outside the school employment office. It was part of his master plan for earning the money to pay for his own car insurance.

After school, the afternoon became one of the longest he'd ever suffered through in his life. He drove from Garden Graphics to Veggie Heaven Produce. From Veggie Heaven Produce to Springtime Flowers. From Springtime Flowers to Deluxe Cleaners. From Deluxe Cleaners to Trendy Threads. He was either too old, too young, the wrong sex (was that legal?), lacking in experience, or one day late. He felt like some kind of outcast.

From the outside, This Town Restaurant looked like the Department of Water and Power. It had a flat gray cement facade. The name was in tiny letters on the door. You either knew the restaurant was there, or you didn't belong.

Inside, the industrial motif continued. Everything was either pink, gray, or black. Structural beams emerged from the walls like the bones of a gigantic animal. The smallest sound made echoes.

Sitting at a tiny round table in back, smoking a cigarette and drinking coffee, was a tightly packed woman with short blond hair. Her name was Cathy Genson, and she owned the joint. She questioned Brandon while with narrow eyes she regarded him through the rising cigarette smoke.

Brandon was so ready for rejection that he was already halfway across the warehouselike room before his brain registered the fact that Cathy Genson had agreed to hire him. Brandon pumped his fist in triumph. Yes!

When Brandon shook her hand enthusiastically, she said, "Overkill, hon," and sipped her coffee.

Brenda had heard about Nitro, of course, but she had always avoided going inside. She could feel the place leeching away her money even though she was just browsing. A music video was playing loudly from a bank of six TV sets hanging from a metal tree at the front of the store. The salesgirls were hip personified. Brenda wondered how they afforded those absolutely rad haircuts on a salesgirl's salary.

Neither Kelly, Tiffany, nor Donna was bothered by the prices or by the fact that even they were dressed somewhat dowdy for this place. Kelly cruised the store, collecting hats, jewelry, dresses, and blouses on her arm, and took everything into a changing room. Donna tried on some tie-dyed shirts that were absolutely sixties. Tiffany put on a very slinky spandex dress—sun yellow for remaining inconspicuous—and preened in front of the mirror as if she were on a fashion-show runway.

Kelly came out of the changing room looking way cool and noted Tiffany. She said to Brenda and Donna, "Tiff has always been so subtle." She pulled a scarf from around her neck and drapped it over Brenda's shoulder. "It's death, Brenda. Positively *you*. One hundred percent silk. You must have it." Brenda looked at the price tag. The national debt. Sure, thought Brenda. She must sprout wings and fly. She must have Vanna White's clothing budget.

She continued to finger the silk scarf—it was very

nice—and said to Kelly, "Do you really think one event can change your life so much?"

Kelly was busy trying on belts. She said, "Sure. Like in *Pretty Woman*."

"No. I mean like Ms. Rye was talking about. Do you think you can do one thing that ruins you forever?"

Brenda could see that as far as this discussion was concerned, Kelly was not even on the same planet. "What?" Kelly asked.

Brenda said, "I don't know. Forget it."

But Tiffany seemed to have been paying attention. She said, "Maybe Jean Valjean wasn't ruined. Maybe he wanted it that way."

Was that possible? Brenda wondered. Could somebody *want* to go to prison? Did motive matter? Was somebody who stole bread less guilty than somebody who stole—she looked around—a hot new broach? Regretfully, she hung the scarf on a hook crowded with scarfs. She said, "Let's get out of here," and walked quickly toward the door. Outside, people passed in the mall. They looked more or less normal. At least they were not so hip she could never hope to compete. The air was not so rarefied.

Tiffany came up next to her and linked arms. "I decided not to buy anything either. Mega-shopper is still in there cleaning out the place." Through the window they could see Donna and Kelly flinging stuff onto the counter and flipping out their credit cards. Brenda didn't even own a credit card, let alone feel free to use one.

But having Tiffany here made her hurt a little less. Maybe she wasn't as wild as Kelly pretended.

14

Get a job

THE NEXT DAY, BRANDON WAS STILL PRETTY
satisfied with himself. Yes, he was. He was ready for
anything This Town or Cathy Genson might throw at
him. Between classes, Steve said to him, "Well, you
scored a sweet job." He shrugged. "If you're into jobs."

Brandon knew that like a lot of guys in Bev Hills,
Steve *wasn't* into jobs. But even Steve's jab couldn't
deflate Brandon's mood.

Dylan joined their knot in the middle of the hallway. Passing kids raced all around them. He said,
"This Town is okay. I ate there opening night." He put
his nose into the air and raised the little finger of one
hand—his tea-drinking hand—and said, "Delicious
cumin."

"Delicious tips, I hope," Brandon said.

"Hey, you're a waiter, dude?"

Steve actually sounded impressed. Brandon liked that. But he didn't want to lie. "I guess. The owner said she was going on instinct."

"I'll bet," Steve said, and wiggled his eyebrows Groucho-style.

Embarrassed, Brandon punched him in the shoulder. Even Dylan laughed.

Just when Brenda thought she was getting a handle on her, Tiffany did something entirely wacko, like strutting up and down the front of Ms. Rye's room in the yellow spandex dress she'd bought at Nitro. Of course, class hadn't begun yet, and she did seem to be getting a lot of attention from the boys, but it still seemed strange to Brenda. She was certain that she never could have done such a thing. From the expression on Kelly's face, *she* did not entirely approve, either. Maybe this was the kind of thing over which she and Tiffany had broken up before.

Ms. Rye came in and Tiffany went to sit down amid applause and catcalls. Brenda had been waiting for a moment like this, when she could speak to Ms. Rye without dangerously looking too interested in class.

Brenda went to stand before her desk. Ms. Rye looked up, a questioning expression on her face, and Brenda said, "I was just wondering. Who's more guilty? Someone like Jean Valjean who didn't want to steal but had to, or"—Brenda lowered her voice, suddenly embarrassed by the personal nature of her question—"or someone who wanted to but didn't?"

Ms. Rye nodded. She seemed pleased. "Interesting moral twister." The bell rang. "We'll deal with it right now."

And they did. But not to Brenda's satisfaction. It seemed that nothing was in black-and-white. Which was more important, action or intent? Could the law-makers ever be more guilty than the lawbreakers? The question of Robin Hood came up, and nobody, not even Ms. Rye, could give an answer that worked *all the time*.

Class happened, and then it was over. The day was over. The week was over. Brenda wanted to get as close to the twilight horseback ride as she could, so she followed Kelly, Donna, and Tiffany to Kelly's lock-er. Brenda saw David Silver coming with his video camera. "Oh no," she said. "Here comes the roving reporter."

David aimed his piece at them and said, "Now a few words from our urban cowgirls."

Giggling, all the girls but Tiffany turned away. She walked slowly toward the camera, swiveling her hips seductively—very effective in that spandex dress. David backed up, but gamely still aimed his camera at her.

Tiffany said, "I'm Tiffany Morgan, and I know what you *really* want to see." With a single swift motion, she pulled off her spandex dress, causing a quick intake of breath from everyone watching, especially David Silver. Under the spandex was a gold lamé body suit. Tiffany walked boldly toward David. He couldn't take the heat anymore and scrammed.

While Tiffany was still enjoying her victory, if that's what it was, Brenda said to Kelly, "What a show."

"Yeah," Kelly said, but she didn't seem happy about it.

Brenda decided she'd never have a better opportunity to get some hard facts about Kelly and Tiffany. She said, "So, why are you guys *ex*-friends?"

The question seemed to make Kelly nervous. Which, Brenda hoped, meant that something really good was coming. But all Kelly said was, "Oh, she was too wild, kind of a troublemaker."

Brenda was going to try again, but Donna got anxious about being late for the ride. Before she allowed herself to be dragged away, Kelly asked if Tiffany was coming.

Tiffany smiled and said, "I have to exchange some stuff. Besides, four-legged creatures don't interest me much."

When Donna and Kelly were gone, Tiffany asked if Brenda wanted to join her at Nitro.

Brenda was delighted by this unexpected bonus of being the only one left for Tiffany to talk to. She tried to sound cool when she accepted.

"Great," said Tiffany. "We can drop by your place on the way."

Huh? Brenda thought.

Shortly after everyone had left, Anna once again arrived at the Walsh home. Once again, Mrs. Walsh tried to get across the fact that Anna was neither wanted nor needed, and once again, Mrs. Walsh found herself on the phone with her husband while Anna cleaned like a whirlwind around her. Once again, the phone cut her off just when Mrs. Walsh felt she was making some headway.

Mrs. Walsh had a cup of coffee—decaf—and offered one to Anna. Anna accepted, and took a few sips, but soon went back to dusting the living room. Mrs. Walsh watched her for a moment and then dug in, too.

Mrs. Walsh knew that her Spanish was even thinner than Anna's English, but she explained out loud, "It's crazy, but I can't watch someone work without helping."

Anna nodded.

"That's why I'm not comfortable with you here. Not you as such, but the idea of you." Mrs. Walsh shook her head and continued trying to explain. Voicing her discomfort with the arrangement helped her, and it didn't seem to bother Anna.

Brenda led Tiffany into the house and in the living room discovered the most humiliating sight she'd ever seen: her mom on the floor, cleaning alongside some Hispanic woman. Brenda thought she would just die. But her mom was looking at them. Surely she expected Brenda to say something.

"That's my mom," Brenda said.

"Which one?" Tiffany whispered.

Brenda smiled as best she could. She was positive that with a personality like Tiffany's, this would be all over school by second period on Monday. As far as Beverly Hills society went, Brenda figured she was dead meat.

"We're going upstairs," Brenda said as she made good speed across the living room to the stairs.

"Sure you don't want a snack?" Mrs. Walsh called after them, sounding slightly frantic.

Brenda had endured enough. She pretended she didn't hear. But even her room was not a safe haven. She died a little more while Tiffany inspected it. It must not be much compared to her room.

Tiffany said, "Okay if I stash some stuff here? I

don't want to lug it around." She glanced into the closet, and Brenda said quickly, "Uh, all my good stuff is in the wash."

Tiffany nodded, apparently willing to believe anything. She actually went into the closet, and for a moment, the half-closed door hid her from Brenda's view. The sooner they were out of here, the better.

Traffic was good to Brandon. Instead of being stuck in Friday traffic hell, he arrived at This Town fifteen minutes early. Cathy Genson seemed surprised but pleased in a vague, noncommittal kind of way. "Let's get busy," she said as she led him across the main dining room.

Brandon didn't know what "let's get busy" meant to Cathy Genson, but at West Beverly High it meant that what followed would probably be X-rated.

That was why, when they entered the deserted kitchen, Brandon said a little nervously, "I thought I was supposed to be a waiter."

Cathy Genson gave a derisive laugh and said, "Babe, you're not waiter material just yet. You'll start with the cumin."

She showed him how to scoop this yellow powder from a big bin into hundreds of tiny shakers. When she left, he tried a little of it on the tip of one finger. It was bitter but the aftertaste reminded him of chili.

Filling the cumin shakers was boring manual work. Brandon figured that he had nowhere to go but up.

As it turned out, he was wrong. In less than an hour, the dining room was full of customers and the kitchen was full of Brandon's fellow workers, all talking to each other in Spanish and a variety of Oriental languages. As far as Brandon could tell, the only workers in the kitchen who could converse in English were himself and a young Vietnamese guy everybody called Chang.

The waiters were men and woman who looked almost as trendy as their customers. Most of them were probably actors waiting for their big break. Brandon had no idea if this was true and he had little chance to find out.

Filling the cumin shakers turned out to be a very minor part of Brandon's job. He was a busboy, and out on the floor he was in great demand. Each waiter expected him to clear his tables *immediately* if not sooner. Brandon worked as fast as he could and still could not satisfy everybody. He held aloft an enormous tray full of dirty dishes and tried to ignore the pain in his wrists. If he kept this up for long, his wrists would have muscles. He'd look like Popeye.

He stood at the enormous stainless-steel sink, scraping dishes with Chang. Brandon tried not to think about what he was doing. Luckily, thinking was not required. Chang told him that Cathy Genson had fired a guy named Julio just before Brandon had arrived. Brandon nodded, understanding at last why he'd been hired so quickly.

Chang said, "She hires, she fires, à la carte. No benefits. Welcome to the Third World."

While he wasn't thinking about his job, Brandon was thinking about the whole This Town scene. There was nothing wrong with honest labor. But he had a bad feeling about Cathy Genson.

They had plenty of time to talk while Tiffany drove them to the mall in her BMW. Probing gently, Brenda said, "So you and Kelly were best friends?"

"Yeah. For two grades. Then she got super possessive and boring."

Tiffany talked about Kelly a little more, all in the
same vein. Her take on their relationship was amazing—certainly very different from Kelly's. Obviously,
point of view was everything.

Inside the mall, Tiffany went straight to Nitro and
stood looking in at the window. Brenda saw the scarf of
her dreams, but still didn't see how she could afford it.
She said, "We were just here yesterday."

As she headed for the door Tiffany said, "That's
the fun: going back."

Brenda didn't quite understand this, but maybe it
didn't matter. She followed Tiffany inside. For a while,
they browsed to the beat of the music video playing on
the six screens. Tiffany called the prices *"freeway rob-
bery."*

Tiffany said, "Hey, Bren, do me a huge favor? Ask
the salesgirl for a smaller size?" She held up a blouse
that seemed to be made of clouds, moonbeams, and
spider silk. Brenda could see right through it.

Tiffany could have done it herself, but Brenda
shrugged and said, "Sure." She went to a salesgirl who
had very red hair and unequal bangs that dangled over
one eye. "Excuse me," Brenda said, "but my friend
needs—" She gestured vaguely in Tiffany's direction.

The salesgirl looked at Tiffany, and her eyes got
wide. Brenda followed her gaze and saw Tiffany stuff a
blue crop top into her backpack. It took a moment for
the full implications of this to strike Brenda. Tiffany
was shoplifting! This was terrible!

Things began to move very slowly, the way they
did during a traffic accident. The salesgirl grabbed

Brenda by the arm and, with her other hand, pushed a button. In an instant, two security guards arrived. One grabbed Tiffany while the other opened the backpack and from it pulled jewelry, the crop top, and the scarf that Brenda had been coveting.

Brenda was about to say something in Tiffany's defense—though she couldn't imagine what—when the salesgirl said, "This one is in on it, too."

"What?" cried Brenda. "Me?" Everybody was looking at her. One of the security guards was putting handcuffs on Tiffany. Brenda had never felt so embarrassed or terrified in her life.

15

Raw deals

BRANDON'S BONES ACHED. HIS MUSCLES ached. His skin ached. The only parts of him that didn't ache were too tired to bother. When he finally pulled Mondale into the driveway, he just sat for a while, listening to the silence.

He dragged himself into the house and discovered that his parents were still up. He collapsed into an armchair while his mom held up a gray-and-white warm-up suit and commented that it seemed a little large for her.

Uncomfortably, his dad said, "Actually, it's for me. I have tennis tomorrow with a client."

Mrs. Walsh looked at him quizzically.

"It's not a couples thing." The admission seemed to embarrass him.

Hoping to save his dad from Mom's burning gaze,

Brandon said, "I'm wiped. And I have to clock in early tomorrow."

Mr. Walsh gratefully began a discussion of how tough his own life had been back in the Stone Age, when he was a kid. "Working *two* jobs, walking miles through the snow, keeping up the old A average, carrying my team to glory—"

"I'm exhausted, too," Mrs. Walsh said, interrupting. "It's tough keeping up with Anna."

"The famous cleaning lady," said Mr. Walsh.

Mrs. Walsh shook her head in admiration. "You know, she's really interesting. She wants to start a business—" She was interrupted by the ringing of the phone.

Mr. Walsh answered it in a jocular tone, but when his face turned grim, his answers became clipped and businesslike. He hung up, seemingly in a state of shock.

"What?" Mrs. Walsh cried. "What?"

Without emotion, Mr. Walsh said, "Brenda has been caught shoplifting."

Mrs. Walsh closed her eyes.

Angrily, Mr. Walsh said, "It has to be that Tiffany she's been hanging around with. You said she had shifty eyes."

"It's all this appearance garbage," Mrs. Walsh said. "Look at you and your warm-up suit. In Minneapolis your old sweats would have been good enough. We're different people here." Mr. and Mrs. Walsh began collecting their keys and coats.

"I don't believe this," Brandon said. "Remember Brenda? Your daughter? The one who made you drive back to St. Paul when she forgot to pay for her Barbie doll?"

Mrs. Walsh shook her head and said again, "We're different people here." She and her husband hurried out the door, leaving Brandon to wonder how different he himself might be.

A security guard cuffed Brenda, too, and took her and Tiffany to a small room at the back of the store. He closed the door and it clicked shut. To Brenda, the click sounded like a prison gate slamming. She was rigid with rage and fear. Her body was filled with it. As she paced from one wall to the other she glared at Tiffany, who seemed unaccountably calm.

Tiffany said, "Relax." She checked her watch. "They have only ten minutes to get us to the police station. If they're late, we can sue for false imprisonment."

Brenda stopped pacing and hugged herself. "Great," she said. "I'm in here with Billy the Kid."

Tiffany came closer to her and said softly, "You know, I stole the scarf for you."

"Give me a break," Brenda said, seething. What made her angrier was that she really did want the scarf.

Tiffany went on. "Hey, I understand that look I saw in your eye. When I'm stealing, it's the only time I feel alive. I can *buy* anything. It's no kick!"

"My heart beats bouillon for you." Brenda turned toward the wall. "Don't talk to me."

"All right," Tiffany said. "I won't talk to you. I'll talk to the owner. And if you want to get out of here, Brenda-the-pure, you better follow my lead."

In a full-length mirror, Brenda saw Tiffany hike up her skirt and knock on the door. A security guard answered it and Tiffany asked to speak with the owner.

A few minutes later the owner came in. He was a bald-ing middle-aged guy who tried to look hip in a blousy white shirt and wide black pants. He wore white socks with his black loafers. From the way he concentrated on Tiffany, hiking up her skirt had been a good idea.

Even through her worry and anger, Brenda admired the slickness with which Tiffany handled the situation. She showed the guy her credit cards—gold cards, most of them—and offered to show him the thousands of dollars' worth of receipts for stuff she'd legally purchased in his store. The clincher was her offering to pay for the stuff found in her backpack. Between the legs and the credit cards and the argu-ments, the guy finally gave in. "Why waste a day in court?" he said.

Brenda was both shocked and relieved at Tiffany's success.

Tiffany left in her BMW, but Brenda had to wait for her parents. The ride home was one of the longest journeys of her life. Most of it was filled with uncom-fortable silences and stony, impassive faces. Tears kept growing in Brenda's eyes and rolling away.

At last, Brenda said, "You guys, I didn't do any-thing wrong. I swear."

Mrs. Walsh, riding shotgun, looked over her shoulder at Brenda. Mr. Walsh said, "If you say so, honey, we believe you."

Sure, Dad, Brenda thought. She shook as she began to cry. "It was awful. I'm so ashamed that you had to come down here and get me. Can't we just for-get it, please?"

After a moment, Mr. Walsh said, "We'll bury it. Case closed."

More time went by. Brenda was very aware that

her mother had not yet said anything. "Mom?" Brenda said.

Mrs. Walsh reached back to grasp her daughter's hand. She said, "Let's go home."

Not really an answer, Brenda noticed. She leaned back in her seat and tried to feel better.

On Saturday morning, Mr. and Mrs. Walsh went out power walking. Mr. Walsh wore his bright, new warm-up suit and Mrs. Walsh strode beside him in her ratty old sweats. She wore them defiantly, like a badge of virtue.

They walked in silence for a long time. Then Mrs. Walsh said, almost to herself, "What if she really did steal?"

Mr. Walsh reached out for his wife's hand and shrugged. He spoke in a placating tone. "Kids steal. It's a stage. You know, they need to get away with something."

Mrs. Walsh nearly smiled when she said, "I was always afraid I'd get caught."

"Well, I confess. I once took a can opener from JC Penny's."

"I don't believe it," Mrs. Walsh said as if she were shocked.

"It's true. When I gave it to my mother, she asked a lot of probing questions and then made me take it back."

"No, Jim. I mean I don't believe Anna showed up on a Saturday."

She had not come to clean, but to deliver a casserole she had made them for dinner. It was a gift. Neither of the Walshes knew what to make of the mys-

terious mixture of sauce and meat, but they thanked
her and took it into the house. Mrs. Walsh put it into
the refrigerator until she felt braver.

Just before the phone went dead and then gave
Brenda a busy signal, Kelly had been explaining that
Tiffany was into all the Os—klepto and nympho for
two. According to Mom, the phone had been on strike
on and off all week. Figures. That was the way
Brenda's life was going at the moment.

While Brenda shook her cordless phone in a useless effort to make it work, Brandon came in and sat
down on the end of her bed. She let the receiver rest in
her lap, and he said, "Feeling better this morning?"

Lightly, she said, "*Les Misérables. C'est moi.*" She
shrugged and felt like crying again. "How could Tiff do
that to me?" The terrible part was that Brenda really
did understand. She wanted things, too. Her list was
different from Tiffany's, but wanting was certainly no
stranger. Somehow, understanding only made the situation worse. She said, "Maybe I should've told on her,
but I just couldn't do it."

Brandon nodded and said. "Hey, it's over."

Easy for you to say, Brenda thought. She would
still have dreams, memories; she'd still see Tiffany in
school. Brenda said, "I got a raw deal."

"Not as raw as some." Brandon looked out the window. He had something on his mind besides her. He
said, "These men I work with are like Grampa was,
coming here from some foreign place with no money,
the language a brick wall." Angrily, he said, "They get
completely exploited."

Sure, Brenda thought. I don't have it so bad. She

shook her head and said, "Look at what's going on here in our own home. Mom hired Anna."

"I'll bet Mom is paying her fairly. The guys at This Town are working for pine nuts."

Brenda didn't find this encouraging. She stared glumly at the carpet.

Brandon went on, "But you know what, Bren? They'll be okay, and so will you."

"I'm okay," she said, hoping it was true. She tried not to think about it, and instead took refuge in the *Les Mis* paper that was due Monday. Her recent adventure with stealing gave her a whole new outlook on it.

Her bedroom was too quiet, too secluded. Being in there was like being in some kind of prison cell. So she went downstairs and plopped herself onto the couch in the living room, where she scribbled on a yellow pad.

Evidently, the phones were working again, because Mom was on one of them dickering for service with the phone company. Anna came in and asked, "Miss Cindy? Me wash?"

Brenda looked up to see what Anna was asking about. The armload of laundry she held had price tags dangling from it.

Oops, Brenda thought as she broke into a cold sweat. She reminded herself firmly that she had nothing to feel guilty about. All of that stuff was probably stolen, certainly from Nitro. Tiffany didn't want to get caught carrying incriminating evidence around at the mall, so she stashed it in Brenda's closet. Anna had found it and was now asking an obvious and innocent question.

As if in a trance, Mrs. Walsh took the clothes from Anna and looked at them. Her eyes grew large as she came to realize what she must be holding. Before Brenda had a chance to explain, Mrs. Walsh threw down the phone and cast an atomic accusing stare at Brenda. So angry she was nearly in tears, Mrs. Walsh rushed from the room still clutching the booty.

Anna looked confused and distraught as Brenda rushed past her. "Mom!" Brenda called. Brandon had been wrong. Her world was falling apart again.

16

Public enemies

FEELING BETRAYED, BRENDA CHASED HER mom upstairs and cornered her at last in her parents' bedroom. Following some weird Mom instinct, she was sorting the stuff into piles on the bed.

"Mom," Brenda cried.

Mrs. Walsh shook a skimpy leather skirt in her face and cried, "Tell me what to think! Please!"

"I could tell you, but I shouldn't have to. And I'm not going to. Go ahead! Think the worst of me." She turned toward the door. Through her jiggling tears it looked like a hundred doors.

Her mom took her by the shoulder and spun her around. Good. They could have it all out here and now. She'd drop out of school and get a job. She'd become a professional thief. She'd—

Mrs. Walsh said, "What you do tell me constantly

is how much you want things. It's all I ever hear." She threw down the leather skirt and went on in a more understanding tone. "Look, it's okay. You went overboard. We can deal with it. We just have to be straight with each other."

"You want straight? I'll give you straight. It's been really hard for me. All I want is to blend in, like I used to in Minneapolis." Almost against her will, she found herself getting angrier. "And not only won't you give me money for the things I need, you go spend money on a maid for yourself!"

"You're not the only one around here without friends, Brenda. At least Anna's someone I can talk with. Well, not exactly with, but—"

Brenda almost smiled at her mom's confusion. Meanwhile, her mom began sorting through the evidence again. She held up a very radical crop top. Like some kind of TV detective, she went on, musing, "You left the price tags on. Maybe you wanted to get caught."

Sounding hysterical, even to herself, Brenda cried, "I'll tell you what I wanted! I wanted to steal. To see my picture on post office walls. To be public enemy number one!"

"Calm down!" Mrs. Walsh cried.

"You calm down! I didn't do it. I couldn't. You should know that. If you don't, you don't know me at all!" She ran out of the bedroom and slammed the door. She had to talk to somebody who could do something about all this. Oddly enough, there was only one person she could go to.

Tiffany's house was far away, and the trip allowed Brenda to walk off some of her anger. But when she saw that the place Tiffany lived was more of a mansion than a house, and how rich and sexy Tiffany looked in the bikini in which she answered the door, Brenda's anger returned. It was no longer a hot anger, though. It was cold enough to make ice cubes.

Tiffany refused to discuss anything till she'd led Brenda through a house that looked like the lobby of some fancy hotel, and into a backyard that was larger than some public parks. Manicured trees stood near an enormous swimming pool.

Tiffany threw herself onto a lounge chair and sipped something tall, green, and cool through a straw. She looked terrific, and Brenda hated her for it.

Brenda told her what had happened.

"What was I supposed to do?" Tiffany asked, attempting to be reasonable. "I couldn't bring the clothes here."

Sarcastically, Brenda said, "It's a crazy notion, I grant you. Guess you don't have the room." She nodded at the trees and the pool, then concentrated on Tiffany again. "Why did you take those things? You have so much."

"You think so?" She glanced at the same things Brenda looked at and obviously saw something else. "Depends on your definition of much. For instance, your mom's the work-it-out type. My folks are never here. At the moment, they're launching a shopping center in Boca Raton." For a moment, Brenda saw a sad, lonely, pitiful little girl. She sat on the chair next to Tiffany. Then the other, hateful Tiffany returned. She said, "It's cool. I do what I want."

"That's cool, yeah." The spell was broken. Brenda's icy anger climbed aboard again. She said, "But this time, because you did what you wanted, my mom thinks I'm a thief."

Tiffany smiled, pitying her.

Brenda said, "You can laugh, but my mom's opinion matters to me."

The smile went away and Tiffany said angrily, "Just go back to Mommy, Brenda. Go back to Minneapolis, okay?"

Brenda did not understand Tiffany's transformation. But she knew she'd been there too long. She said, "Fine. Just fine," and started her long walk home.

Brandon had never before seen a crew of workmen digging into a perfectly good street. They would have their reasons, of course, but what mattered to Brandon was the fact that where three lanes had been the day before, there was now only one. The traffic was surreal.

Cathy Genson docked him for being ten minutes late, though he'd been fifteen minutes early the day before. But the evening was young yet.

As This Town crowded up Brandon's evening became crazier. Many waiters paid more attention to customers who were agents or producers than they did to civilians. Brandon found himself smoothing ruffled feathers despite Cathy Genson's constant reminder that "crumbers never talk to customers." Other waiters expected him to be in two places at once.

"Yo, boy!"

Brandon turned around, ready to explode, when he saw that the person who'd called him was Dylan. Brandon the crumber smiled and made his way between tables while Dylan read aloud from the menu in an affected English accent. "This Town, not just a restaurant, but an eating experience." Dylan was very good. Brandon was enjoying himself for the first time in hours. "Sage, cumin, bouquets of fragrant ve-ge-table jewels—"

Cathy Genson pulled Brandon aside and said angrily, "Remember what I said about crumbers and customers. Many people would love to have your job, babe."

As Cathy Genson crossed the room to a newly arrived customer she opened wide her arms, smiled, and cried, "Darling!" Chang approached, and together, he and Brandon watched Cathy Genson showboat across the crowded room.

"Love that minimum wage," Brandon said.

Chang looked at him with astonishment and said, "You get minimum wage? Congratulations, man. The rest of us get whatever La Genson feels like paying."

Brandon's bad feeling quickly took on form. "That's illegal."

"Right," said Chang. "Who among us is gonna blow the whistle?"

Brandon realized that Chang was right. For Chang and the others, working at Cathy Genson's joint was how they ate and paid their rent. Even a bad gig was better than no gig at all. Brandon was just looking for a way to pay his own car insurance. Somebody had to do something, and it looked as if he was elected.

He made his way across the room to where Cathy Genson was laughing with a very distinguished man in a Camp Beverly Hills T-shirt and jogging pants. Brandon tapped Cathy Genson on the shoulder and said, "Excuse me—"

Without looking in his direction, Cathy Genson said, "I loathe apologies, Brendon. Make it up to me. The cumins need filling."

This was *it,* Brandon thought. Loud enough for half the room to hear, he said, "The name is Brandon. Brandon Walsh. I'm an investigative reporter for the West Beverly High School newspaper."

"That's great, Brendon. You're fired." She turned away from him.

He grabbed her by the shoulder and turned her around again. "You can ignore me now, but lots of parents read that paper, and some of them eat here. They won't like hearing that your help is getting less than minimum wage."

Brandon was aware that except for one person applauding, the place was dead silent. He looked away from Cathy Genson's amazed face and saw the person making the noise was Dylan. Brandon took off his busboy jacket and laid it across a tray of dirty dishes. As he walked toward Dylan, conversation started again. He was gratified to notice that some people were leaving.

"Can we go somewhere else?" Brandon said.

"Gotcha, man," Dylan said as he stood up. "I know just the place."

They went out to the Porsche, and Dylan drove Brandon across town. Explaining as much to himself as to Dylan, Brandon said, "I don't just need to support my car insurance habit. My dad's always worked, and—"

"Minnesota, you worry too much."

Dylan told him that they were going to the Peach Pit Diner. It was owned and operated by Nat Pitluck, a former character actor who made the best peach pie in town.

The Peach Pit was a small unpretentious joint—a joint in the best sense of the word—at the edge of

Beverly Hills. Nat was a lumpy, fiftyish guy in a white apron and a paper hat. He wasn't one of the beautiful people, but everything about him was real, including his peach pie.

Brandon and Dylan sat at the counter. Brandon goggled at the mound of pie and ice cream Nat placed before him. Dylan dug into his, and Brandon wasn't far behind. Great pie—firm peaches, not too much sugar, light flaky crust. Great pie.

"Real food for real people," Dylan said.

"Damn straight," said Nat. "Take it or leave it."

The coffee was good, too—fresh, and strong enough to grow hair on rocks. While Brandon took another sip, Nat wiped down the counter and studied him.

Nat said, "Dylan here's been bugging me to hire someone to help me. But I figure, who'd be nuts enough to want *this* gig?"

Brandon saw what was happening and he spoke up before it stopped. "Me! Take me! I'm nuts enough."

"It's true," Dylan said.

Nat nodded and stuck his hand across the counter. Brandon took it and they shook. The pie, the coffee, the job! Life was good.

Brenda was in her room writing about the moral questions in *Les Misérables*. In the last few days, stealing had become a very personal subject, and she had no trouble thinking of things to say about it. The front doorbell rang downstairs. A moment later, Brenda heard the voice of Tiffany Morgan. She stiffened. Hadn't that girl caused enough trouble?

17

Hungers

BRENDA CREPT OUT OF HER ROOM AND ALONG
the hallway to the top of the stairs. Mom was below
speaking to Tiffany, who was still outside. Tiffany
looked fairly spectacular in a hot-pink jumpsuit with
gold buckles. After all her trouble lately, Brenda tried
not to covet it too much.

Tiffany said, "I just came to get the stuff I left over
here."

"I'm afraid I don't—"

"You know: the goods; the contraband; the price
tags. Remember?"

Brenda couldn't see her mom's face, but Mom's
entire body seemed to relax. Brenda wiped a tear from
her eye. She was crying again. Not from anger this
time, but from gratitude.

While Mrs. Walsh went to get the clothes Tiffany

came into the house. Brenda was afraid she would steal something, but all she did was stare longingly at the family photographs on the wall. Mrs. Walsh returned with the stolen stuff and handed them to Tiffany. "I assume these are going back where they came from?" And then, more warmly, went on, "Tiffany, I know I'm not your parent—"

"That's right. You're not." Tiffany sounded more sorry than sarcastic. She set the evidence down on a small table near the door.

Good old Mom just forged ahead. She said, "But I think maybe you should speak to someone about this stealing business."

Tiffany ran her finger down the side of a photograph of Brenda and her mom. She said, "My parents don't have time. They just off me onto shrinks. The shrinks tell me I'm just trying to get my parents' attention. A vicious circle." Tiffany shrugged and walked out the door. She turned at the step and said. "I just wanted you to know it was me, not Brenda. Your daughter's cool. You ought to warn her about people like me."

As Tiffany walked to her car Mrs. Walsh waved the goods in the air and called, "Hey, you forgot—"

Without turning around, Tiffany called back, "Keep it!"

Crying now for sure, Brenda heard an engine start, and then her mom closed the door. Seconds later, they were in each other's arms, both crying and apologizing and promising to trust each other forevermore.

Brenda brought her books downstairs and worked on her *Les Mis* paper. Mrs. Walsh did a little sewing. They didn't talk much, but the silence was cheerful and relaxed.

Later, Brandon came home bragging about how Dylan had helped him get a new improved new job. When he had run out of superlatives to describe the

Peach Pit, he asked Brenda how her day had gone.

"Cool," she said with enthusiasm. "I was accused, unaccused, self-accused, fought with Mom, and lost a friend. But you know, I finished reading a pretty good book."

Brandon picked up the neat stack of paper next to her, and as if he were reading a speech, read out loud:

"'Many of us have had the urge to steal, but Jean Valjean actually acted on that urge. Jean Valjean stole because he was hungry for food. Others steal because they have different kinds of hunger.'"

Mrs. Walsh looked up from her sewing and smiled at Brenda. "I'm sorry I jumped to conclusions, dear. I should know you well enough to trust you." Still smiling, she turned to Brandon and said accusingly, "You, on the other hand—"

"Please," said Brandon. "I'm reading." He made a big production out of clearing his throat, and went on:

"'There's the hunger to belong. There's emotional hunger. People with the hunger to be loved or needed or just noticed require understanding. They can show greatness by not letting other people take the rap for their crimes. Other kinds of hunger include—'"

Mr. Walsh came into the kitchen saying, "The hunger of a father who went to a fancy tennis match where they served nothing but the chintziest little— you couldn't even call them sandwiches."

He opened the refrigerator and frowned while he studied the interior.

Mrs. Walsh suggested, "You could try Anna's mystery casserole."

The casserole was heating on the stove, but no one had had the nerve to actually try it. Mr. Walsh decided to be brave. He found a wooden spoon in the drawer and was looking for a good place to stick it in.

"Don't talk to me about food," Brandon said. "I ate at both my jobs." He realized something and perked up. "Hey, Dad! I had *two* jobs today and drove through miles of asphalt. Not bad, huh?"

Mr. Walsh was still investigating the interior of Anna's casserole. "Way to go, Brandon," he said. He put in the spoon, and then lifted sauce to his mouth. He smiled and handed the spoon to his wife. She smiled, too. "Way to go, Anna," Mr. and Mrs. Walsh said together.

The good feelings seemed to disappear along with Anna's casserole. The next morning, the twins were late getting rolling because Brandon and their father decided to shoot baskets in the driveway before school.

This circumstance gave Brenda the chance to point out once again to her mother that she could not depend on Brandon for transportation. She really needed her own car.

"You need a driver's license first, honey," Mrs. Walsh said.

"I'm taking driver's training."

"I know. And I'm praying we'll all"—she searched for a diplomatic phrase—"get through it this time."

Brenda began to explain what had happened those other times, but was interrupted by Brandon honking Mondale's horn.

The drive to school did not improve Brenda's

mood. It seemed to her that Brandon drove too slowly and did not take sufficient advantage of his opportunities to change lanes.

"What is your problem this morning?" he asked.

Wheels, or the lack of them, was her problem. "Just drive," she said. "Okay?"

Once they got to school, things improved a little. She found Kelly and Donna right away and so had a chance to practice the latest hip lingo.

"Kelly," said Brenda.

"So. Brenda," said Kelly.

"So. Late."

"So. New?"

Brenda shook her head and fingered Kelly's shirt. "So. Cute," she said enthusiastically.

"So. Thanks."

"So. Bye-yee," said Brenda.

"So. Bye-yee," said Kelly.

"So. Bye-yee," said Donna.

When Brandon told Andrea that he was going out for the team as well as covering the basketball tryouts for the *Blaze,* she seemed surprised. "Aren't you a little short?" she asked.

"Thanks for the vote of confidence," Brandon said.

Now, sitting on the bench to wait for his turn, Brandon decided that Andrea had known something he hadn't. These guys were humongous. According to Steve, DeWitt was six-foot-six and never missed a shot. Clinton was only six-four, but played defense, as Steve so delicately put it, "like King Kong." Walker was better than both of them.

In the middle of it all was Coach Reilly, a handsome middle-aged man with iron-gray hair and a whistle around his neck. He was the conductor, the ringmaster, the big kahuna.

Steve continued to talk while he stretched. "West Beverly is the perennial powerhouse. League champs four years in a row."

"A winning team brings out the hopefuls, I guess." Brandon looked around at the crowd of benchwarmers.

Steve smiled cynically. "These open tryouts are so bogus. Coach Reilly only holds them to promote school spirit. Everyone knows he's already set the lineup." Steve leaned closer and spoke in a normal voice, which in that huge gym had the effect of whispering. "For instance, he told me I'm practically a lock."

"I guess I'll try out anyway."

Steve looked at Brandon with surprise and said, "Aren't you kind of short?"

Brandon just shook his head and concentrated on maintaining his confidence. And it took a lot of maintaining. Coach Reilly obviously had his favorites, and everybody else was just there to prevent the bench from floating away. Clinton, Walker, and DeWitt made swift music on the court. A big black guy named James Townsend was no slouch either. That left one space open on the lead five, and Brandon had little hope of filling it, especially if Steve's theories about tryouts were correct.

Then Brandon had his chance to play, and he forgot his doubts and fears in the excitement of moving the ball around. He may have been short, but his body knew what it was doing. That was all that counted. A few times, he got ahold of the ball and shot it to Townsend. Townsend dunked it every time. They were good together.

Evidently, Brandon's feelings were not an illusion. Coach Reilly called to him and asked his name. Brandon took that as a good sign. He ignored the dirty look Steve gave him. No point losing a friend over a basketball game.

Having won the big stock-car race for the fifth year in a row, Brenda Walsh, idol of millions, rolled down her window, shook her terrific hair out of her helmet, and said to the camera, "Porsche. Not just car, but a way of life."

"Brenda Walsh."

It took a moment for Brenda to readjust to reality. Mr. Karton, the driver's training teacher, had called her name. He was nice, even if he dressed in plaids and his bow tie bobbed when he spoke. He had big round glasses and a constant nervous smile.

When she tried to explain about her previous exploits in other driver's training classes, he assured her that as far as he was concerned, everybody started with a clean slate. "Who cares if you flunked driver's training once before?"

Mr. Karton really was very nice and so she felt that she had to be honest. Painfully honest, if necessary. "Twice before," Brenda said. "Three times if you count the first time, but I only lasted twenty minutes, so I really don't think it should count. Do you, Mr. Karton?"

Mr. Karton continued to smile, but it was a long time before he said, "Let's see what happens, shall we?"

He took Brenda and three other students out to a very plain vanilla kind of car parked in front of the school. After he showed them the tires and the gas cap and things like that, they went for a ride. Driving with those other students was no worse than driving with Brandon.

When it was her turn behind the wheel, Brenda felt in her pocket for her key chain. It had a fluffy pink pom-pom, and Brenda had bought it at Farmer's Market as kind of an investment in the future. At the moment, nothing was attached to it. But when she got her own car, she planned to hang the keys from it.

She let go of the key chain and then concentrated hard on what she was doing. She wanted to do well, not only for herself, but for Mr. Karton.

"How do you feel?" Mr. Karton asked.

"Like I could do this even if you weren't sitting next to me." This was great, Brenda thought. From here to the Grand Nationals was a small step, a short drive. She and the pink pom-pom would do it together.

"Of course you can," said Mr. Karton. "And you will. All right, let's take the big wide turn."

Carefully, Brenda turned the wheel. The car made a big circle across the deserted parking lot. There were no cars to run into, but she didn't want to run into one of the light posts either.

Quite a crowd gathered outside the gym. The guys waited with exaggerated nonchalance when Coach Reilly came out to post the names of those who'd survived the first cut. When Coach Reilly went back into his office, the crowd rushed the bulletin board.

As guys who didn't find their names walked away in disappointment, Brandon and Steve wormed their way to the front. They marveled at the list.

Steve said, "I don't believe it."

"There has to be some mistake," Brandon said. "I was hoping we'd get to play together this season."

Steve ran his finger up and down the list again. His

name was not there. For some reason, Brandon felt that by making the team, he'd betrayed a friend. He shrugged off the feeling. It obviously wasn't true.

Angrily, Steve said, "If you think you're going past the next round, you're totally naive. The whole thing is totally bogus, anyway."

"What do you mean, bogus?" Brandon asked.

"You know how many of those basketball-playing machines live in Beverly Hills?"

Brandon raised his eyebrows and waited.

"A big fat zippo." Steve held up his fingers to make a goose egg.

Brandon was feeling pretty good about making the cut, but the entire situation was taking an unsavory turn. That is, if he wasn't just the target of the famous Steve Sanders paranoia. He said, "Wait a minute, Steve. I thought you couldn't go to West Beverly unless you lived in the district." Andrea's face flashed across his mind. He told himself that was different.

"Sure," said Steve. "Unless you're a major jock. Then they insert you into that Applied Learning Opportunity thing."

"Applied what?"

"It's supposed to be a special program for minorities. So we can all become more enriched and diverse." Steve wasn't just angry now, he was bitter. "But in reality, the major requirement is that you need to jump higher or run faster than anybody else. And after you've been here awhile, you might notice that these suckers never go to class."

DeWitt, Walker, and Townsend made a lot of noise as they came out of the locker room. Brandon contemplated them and wondered, his own paranoia barely under control, if Steve's ugly little accusation was even remotely correct.

18

It's a duck

KELLY CAME OVER FOR DINNER BECAUSE SHE and Brenda were going to study Spanish after. But first, Brenda had to live through the meal, which might not be possible because Dad was in coach mode. Brenda always hated Dad's rah-rah speeches, especially when he made them in front of her guests. And it was all for Brandon's benefit, anyway. And of all the people she knew, Brandon needed rah-rah speeches least.

"You can't let a little competition get you down," Dad said.

Brandon became very excited. He made large fish motions with his hands and said, "Little? The starting five is right out of *Land of the Giants*."

Brandon claimed that Dad's pep talks didn't bother him, but Brenda suspected they did. They made

Brandon feel anxious about doing well, and nobody needs that noise.

Brenda and Kelly managed to survive dinner. "Bye-yee," quoth Brenda to her mother as she and Kelly escaped upstairs.

As Brenda had expected, Spanish was not to be the main topic of the evening. The main topic was a blind date Kelly wanted to set Brenda up with. Kelly's date swore that his friend was a dream, but both Kelly and Brenda knew that Kelly's date, Kenny, was no bargain himself.

"Then why would you want to go out with him again?" Brenda asked. She looked over the top of her open Spanish book to Kelly, who was applying a very hot shade of blue nail polish.

"Because," Kelly said as if she were revealing a secret of the universe, "Kenny and his friend are getting front row tickets to the Janet Jackson concert. And they're renting a limo. And it'll be fun. What do you say, *amigo?*

"That's *amiga,*" Brenda said, but otherwise did not commit to anything.

Brandon liked tech class, but he was always a little nervous around Ms. Yamado. She was friendly and helpful, but she also knew everything. He was working on his video camera when James Townsend came in looking a little sheepish. When Ms. Yamado asked if he'd had a chance to do his assignment, Brandon knew *why* he looked sheepish.

"I'm still working on it. And I'll have it for you Monday. For sure. Really."

Ms. Yamado gave him a break and moved on. She generally gave people breaks till doing it no longer made sense.

Brandon said, "I didn't know you were taking tech."

"Well, I'm enrolled in it," Townsend said. "But you know how it is coming to a new school and all."

Brandon gave him a polite smile. He knew exactly how it was coming to a new school. He'd done it himself only four weeks before. And he still managed to get his assignments in on time. Could Steve be right about the Applied Learning Opportunity program?

Brandon cornered Andrea in the *Blaze* office and told her what he'd observed and how it seemed to jibe with what Steve Sanders had told him.

With some sarcasm, Andrea said, "The fact is, the ALOP has a great reputation. Another fact is that Steve Sanders is a spoiled slug who is not even close to being a credible news source."

Brandon knew investigative journalism was sometimes difficult, but he hadn't supposed the trouble would start with his editor. His disappointment must have shown on his face because Andrea said, "Look, if you think there's a major news story here, set up some interviews and go for it."

"I can't write this. If I make the team, it's a blatant conflict of interest. If I don't, it looks like sour grapes."

"If it looks like a duck, and quacks like a duck—"

"You don't think it's unfair they bring a guy in from out of district to play basketball?"

Andrea looked down. Without meaning to, Brandon had apparently struck a chord. He knew that Andrea was in a similar situation. He said, "This isn't about geography."

"Right. It's about race."

Brandon felt as if Andrea had slapped him. What did she make him out to be, anyway? He said, "Forget it," and turned away.

"If you really think there's a story here, give me a few names and I'll see what dirt I can dig up at the ALOP office."

Brandon nodded. This could be good.

At practice, Brandon moved the basketball around pretty good. It was true, Walker, DeWitt, and Townsend seemed to protect each other no matter which team they were on, but Brandon managed to hold his own. Then his father showed up to watch and Brandon's concentration fell to pieces.

His father claimed he was there because a meeting in Century City had broken up earlier than expected. But Brandon still didn't feel good about his dad talking to Coach Reilly. It looked too much like Dad was asking for favors. Dad never would, of course. Brandon didn't think he would.

Dad finally left, and Brandon felt better. Parents hanging around school always made him nervous. Andrea caught up with Brandon at his locker. And she had big news. The ALOP office had no record of James Townsend ever taking a reading or a math placement test—something every sophomore on campus had to go through.

"I knew it," Brandon said.

"It gets worse. His transcript from his last school somehow never got processed, so he's the only student at West Beverly without a grade-point average."

"Gotcha," Brandon said. This could be really big. It could break the school wide open.

Andrea volunteered to speak with Townsend, but her heart wasn't in it. So Brandon said that he would.

He found Townsend, DeWitt, and Walker on the front lawn pretending they were the Harlem Globetrotters. When Townsend agreed to speak with

Brandon alone, DeWitt and Walker split. Brandon and Townsend sat down on a bench. Townsend made baby bounces between his feet with the basketball. Even just sitting around, Townsend was an enormous guy.

Townsend said, "I saw that little bump-and-run Walker laid on you during practice, and I told him it was a cheap shot. But he's just looking out for me because I'm the new kid on the block. That's all it is. Understand?"

Brandon understood. Quietly, he said, "A lot of people are looking out for you, aren't they, James?"

Townsend smiled and shook his head. "I guess they are."

Brandon was rapidly beginning to like Townsend, and that wouldn't be good for the story. Suddenly all business, Brandon said, "Look, I'm the sports editor of the *Beverly Blaze*.

"The school paper?"

"That's right. And we have reason to believe that you have been recruited to play basketball here in exchange for certain special privileges." He said "special privileges" as if they had quotes around them.

"Say what?" Townsend said, absolutely incredulous. He held the baskeball in one big hand.

"Come on, James. You live out of district. You never go to class. And I understand your transcript doesn't list any prior grades, or test scores, or anything to indicate that you even have the minimum requirements to be in this school. Or any school, for that matter."

Townsend stood up slowly and the hand that wasn't holding the ball made a fist. He didn't hold it up or threaten Brandon with it, but Brandon knew it was there. "Who gave you the right to be poking around my records?" he said.

"That's not the—"

"It *is* the issue. If I was white, you would not be doing this." His anger was under pressure, ready to explode at any moment.

Brandon was getting pretty angry himself. Townsend was the second person today to accuse him of being some kind of Nazi. Brandon thought of himself as a bleeding-heart liberal. The racist stuff did not go down well. He said, "I don't care if you're white or black or blue with little orange polka dots. You shouldn't be here on a free pass."

The fist came up now, shaking. Seemingly through an act of will, Townsend put it down. He just said, "Yeah. Right," and walked away quickly.

Brandon called after him, "The truth is going to come out, James."

Townsend kept walking.

19

The late shift

LUCKILY, BRENDA HAD GOTTEN A RIDE HOME with Kelly. On this particular occasion, Brandon knew that he was not a sterling example of the classic careful driver. He was preoccupied with thoughts about Townsend and about Andrea and about the difference between them. Townsend was black and Andrea was white. But there was more to it than that. If Brandon was going to continue living in his skin, there had to be.

After a long hard think, Brandon decided that the main difference was that Andrea had come to West Beverly for herself, to get the best education possible. Once one got past the little deception she had perpetrated to get in, she took the same classes, fulfilled the same academic requirements as everybody else.

On the other hand, Townsend had been drafted only to bring glory to the school. Education was a secondary consideration, if it entered into the equation at all.

Brandon felt better after he'd laid all this out, but he still could not help suspecting that a double standard was in action here, and he didn't like it.

When he got home, Brandon found Brenda simultaneously taking a pizza from the microwave and hanging up the phone. She told him about the date Kelly and Kenny had planned for that night. The phone call had been Kelly's last-ditch effort to convince Brenda to come along. Wisely, as far as Brandon was concerned, Brenda had declined. Though she had sighed. "They *are* renting a limo."

"Speaking of limos, how's driver's training?"

Brenda used a fork to pick up strings of cheese from the pizza. Without looking at him, she said, "Great. Except I had a little accident."

"How little?"

"I crunched a fender on Henry Winkler's car."

"You ran into the Fonz?"

Brenda went on hurriedly, "If Mr. Karton hadn't pointed him out, I never would have even seen him. Tell Mom and Dad, and you're history."

"Who's paying for the body work?"

"The school has insurance."

"Your secret is safe with me."

As Brandon went to change for his shift at the Peach Pit, Brenda said, "Careful up there. Dad found his yearbook in the garage."

Brandon made the proper grimace. He liked to hear the old stories almost as much as Dad liked to tell them, but he'd be late if Dad really got into gear. The yearbook indicated that he probably would. Brandon had to be careful. Still, when Dad invited him into the bedroom, Brandon was unable to decline.

Mom found them marveling over the photograph of Dad's basketball team, the one that had beaten Franklin for the championship. She looked terrific in a party dress and about half the makeup Brenda would have used. Mr. Walsh looked up at her and blinked. "How did it get to be so late?"

"Time flies when you're double-dribbling down memory lane."

Brandon smiled as his dad slunk off to the bathroom. "You look great, Mom," Brandon said.

"I'm glad somebody noticed," Mrs. Walsh said. She spoke a little loudly and leaned toward the bathroom. More conversationally, she asked, "What time will you be home tonight?"

"I don't know. I'm on the late shift."

Mr. Walsh's voice echoed from the bathroom. "Final tryouts are tomorrow, and you're working the late shift?"

"It's for a good cause, Dad—my car insurance."

After a moment, Mr. Walsh called, "If you make the team, we might be able to arrange a little subsidy."

"For real?"

"Absolutely."

"Jim," said Mrs. Walsh, "that's bribery."

Mr. Walsh stuck his head out of the bathroom. His face was half-covered in shaving cream. "Not really. In my humble opinion, student athletes deserve a little bonus for putting in all those extra hours."

I'm just a high-school kid, Brandon thought. I need some guidance here. If Dad pays my car insurance, is it bribery or a bonus?

When Mr. Walsh was safely back in the bathroom, Mrs. Walsh pretended to be speaking to Brandon, but she spoke too loudly, and mostly for her husband's benefit. She said, "Do yourself a favor, Brandon. Do not under any circumstances ever again listen to anything that man says." She leaned toward the bathroom. "Do you hear me, Brandon?"

Still dizzy from being at the center of his parents' disagreement, he said, "I have to go get ready for work," and left the room.

Brandon left for work, and Mr. and Mrs. Walsh left for the party. Brenda's nightmare began shortly thereafter. It began with the ringing of the telephone.

"Hello?" Brenda said.

"Brenda. You must rescue me."

It was Kelly, and she sounded frantic. Brenda said, "Where are you?"

"In hell. Janet Jackson has laryngitis, Kenny is drunk and puking all over the limo, and you must come get me."

"Gross. Can't you take a cab?"

"I'm hanging up now. Have a nice life." She did not hang up. Far away, behind Kelly, Brenda could hear heavy hits playing.

A friendship shouldn't end this way. Kelly would have to see reason. Brenda said, "You know I don't have a California driver's license."

"But you're a good driver, right? That's what you said, right?"

Right. Sure. Brenda tried to remember what else she'd told Kelly on this subject. There seemed to be no way out. She said, "Brandon rode his bike. I guess I could borrow his car."

"You'll be back in ten minutes, max. I promise. Who else can I call? You're my best friend."

"I am?" Doomed, thought Brenda.

Kelly was at Entre Nous, a hot new club at the corner of Doheny and Melrose. Not far. Too far. For luck, Brenda attached Brandon's keys to the pink pom-pom key chain. She went outside, got Mondale started, and backed out of the driveway. "Good old Mondale," she said as if the car were a horse. "Good old Mondale."

There wasn't much traffic, but it was all hideous. People kept honking and going around her. Cross traffic kept almost hitting her. She fingered her pom-pom and spoke out loud to reassure herself. "Honk if you're obnoxious," she yelled to a set of taillights. "I'm a good driver," she told herself. "I'm a great driver." She wished her dad was there to give her a pep talk. She wished her dad was there driving the car.

Then the car wasn't going at all. Suddenly the engine just cut out. Maybe she was about to be picked up by a UFO. That would be great. She'd never have to face Kelly or Brandon. But her problem was not a UFO. Mondale was just out of gas. It rolled to a stop, stranding her in the middle of an intersection.

Well, that was it. Things could get no worse. She walked toward downtown Beverly Hills, the location of that funky gas station with the big saddle-shaped roof. And it was open! Her luck was changing.

The attendant was kind of cute. The stitching on his pocket said his name was Hal. And he was perfectly willing to sell her gas. And he would need two dollars for the deposit on the gas can.

It was at that moment Brenda discovered that things could get worse. She had remembered her pom-pom, but she had forgotten her wallet. She would be without a license even if she owned one.

"These things happen," Hal said understandingly.

He was so understanding that he agreed to take some gasoline and drive her back to Mondale. She almost kissed him, but she controlled herself. He might get the wrong idea.

They got into the tow truck and Hal drove them to where Brenda had left the car. Hal was a very good driver. When they got to the place, Brenda discovered that even at this stage, things could get worse yet. She said, "I don't believe this."

"Where's the car?" Hal asked.

It wasn't there. Brenda was sure they were at the right intersection. It just wasn't there. "My brother is going to kill me," Brenda said.

Hal shrugged. "Tell him these things happen."

Brenda knew that Brandon would not share Hal's outlook.

20

Too many assumptions

AS IT TURNED OUT, BRANDON'S EVENING WAS also not exactly a slice of heaven. He barely escaped from Nat—who was giving lessons in sandwich construction—in time to make it to the library before closing. He returned his books at the desk and looked around to see who else was there. He saw James Townsend laboring over a table full of open books and making hurried notes.

Brandon walked over to his table and, in an astonishing display of diplomacy, asked, "What are you doing here?"

Townsend didn't even look up. He continued writing and said, "I don't have to justify myself to you."

He's angry and he doesn't like me, Brandon thought. He could kill me with one finger. If I'm smart, I'll fold my tent and steal silently away. But where

would high-school journalism be if I did that? Brandon
said, "If you would have answered my questions about
the Applied Learning Opportunity program—"

Townsend exploded in his face. He said, "How the
hell should I know about the ALOP? I'm not in it!"

The phrase "circumstantial evidence" did the back-
stroke through Brandon's brain. He's not in the program. That's why the office didn't have his records.
Simple. Straight forward. And very embarrassing. It
hadn't even occurred to Brandon. Surprised and horrified at his own presumption, Brandon said, "You
weren't recruited at West Beverly to play basketball?"

"That's right," Townsend said sarcastically. His
entire posture was somehow sarcastic.

Trying to get a handle on the situation, Brandon
asked, "But you don't live in the district, do you?"

"Caught me red-handed."

"Then how did you get permission to go to school
in Beverly Hills?"

When Townsend spoke, he sounded very tired, as
if the weight of all his people's sorrows were on his
back. But what he said gave him strength and goaded
him to rightous anger. "I don't need permission. My
father has worked for the Beverly Hills city library for
fifteen years! That gives me as much right to be here
as anybody. Including you!"

His last sentence was a shout, and they attracted
the attention of the librarian, who threw them both out.
"Closing time anyway," she said.

They went outside, and Townsend walked away.
Brandon stopped and said, "I don't know what to say."

Townsend whirled on Brandon like a cornered animal. "Then why don't you try saying nothing for a
change? I was getting by just fine in Inglewood when

my parents decided it was time to upgrade my education. Yeah, four weeks into the semester. I was playing catch-up from the git-go."

Brandon smiled and, almost to himself, said, "That's kind of what happened to me."

"Sure," said Townsend, exploding again. "But you be a white boy so everythin' be coo'. You scope my black skin and you think, he dumb, or he a rap singer, or he in a gang, or he smokin' crack, or whatever stereotype fits your fears." Suddenly the ghetto accent was gone. "But that's your problem, Walsh. And if I use my God-given talents to get into the college of my choice, what's it to you? I have nothing to hide, nothing to be ashamed of, and nothing more to say to you. Ever."

Townsend walked into the night, leaving Brandon to feel like the biggest doofus who ever lived. The feeling stayed with him for the entire ride home. Brandon feared that it would stay with him forever. He was just glad that he could work his anger and frustration out on a bike ride. He arrived home in record time only to discover more horrors waiting for him.

A stranger in a gray suit stood in the kitchen speaking with his parents and his sister. Dad gave Brandon the bad news.

"Somebody stole Mondale?" Brandon said with disbelief. The perfect end to a perfect day.

The man in the gray suit, who had been introduced as Detective Kenner, said, "It was a professional job. They must have come up the driveway."

Brandon shook his head. "Why would anybody in Beverly Hills want a 1983 bomber?"

Kenner shrugged. His concern was professional but no more. "South of the border, a power engine in good condition can bring three times its market value."

Brenda said she was sorry. Brandon was too much in shock to be gracious.

In his conciliatory-father voice, Dad said, "It's late. I suggest we all go to bed and in the morning give this problem our best shot."

The frustration left over from his conversation with Townsend fired Brandon. His anger at being such a jerk fanned the flames. This rah-rah stuff was a pain. Brandon said, "And what if I don't give it my best shot, Dad?"

Mr. Walsh seemed surprised by the question, and then he misunderstood. He said, "Like I said, if you don't make the team, the sun still shines, the moon still—"

"No," said Brandon hotly. "Suppose I don't try out tomorrow. What if I quit right now?"

Entirely bewildered, Mr. Walsh said, "What's the problem, Brandon? We'll find you a different car—"

"I'm not talking about cars."

"I just assumed—"

"You just assumed," Brandon said. He heard the sarcasm in his voice, but couldn't stop it. Maybe he didn't even want to stop it. He'd had a tough evening. "You assumed I wanted a different car. You assumed I wanted to play high-school basketball. You assumed I wanted to move to Beverly Hills. But you never asked for my opinion any more than you asked Mom if she wanted a maid. You just believed everything was cool because that's what you wanted to believe. Guess again, Dad."

Brandon was aware he'd made a fool of himself with his pretentious speech. And he also knew it hadn't been his dad he'd been lecturing to. He'd been lecturing to himself. Brandon Walsh, doofus investigative reporter, convicted of assuming in the first degree. But he was too tightly wound to explain right now. He just left the kitchen as quickly as he could. Shocked by his outburst, no one stopped him.

Later, after he'd cooled down a little, Brandon went to his parents' room to apologize. He found Brenda just outside the open door, eavesdropping on a conversation. Brandon stopped behind Brenda and listened, too. Apparently, Mom was less confused by his outburst than Dad had been. She understood Brandon's need for more emotional space, and with a little explaining, she convinced Dad of it, too. Mom and Dad were no worse than Brandon was. They were just human.

Brandon touched Brenda's shoulder and she jumped. He pulled her back to her room and closed the door. Something had been bothering him, and he let her know what it was. He asked, "When they came down the driveway to steal the car, why didn't you hear anything?"

Brenda gave him her cute nervous smile, calculated to defuse his anger. But she was too late. Brandon was too wrung out to be angry. Now he was only curious.

"It wasn't exactly stolen from the driveway," Brenda said.

Confused, Brandon said, "I'm sure there's a fascinating story here someplace."

Frantically, Brenda tried to explain. "Kelly needed a ride home from the Date from Hell, and she said I'd be back in ten minutes, and who knew Mondale was low on gas?"

"You took my car without asking me?"

"You're right to be angry, Brandon. You are. I'll pay you back if I have to baby-sit for centuries. Really. Just don't tell Mom. Please."

"Tell her what? That you took my car or that you lied to her about it?"

Brenda cleverly changed the subject. Knowing

that it was pointless to pin her down, Brandon let her. Defensively, she said, "I didn't know Mondale was going to strand me."

"Did you check that thing on the dash, Brenda? You know, the gas gauge?"

Brenda bit her lip, and then suddenly said joyously, "It's all the fault of Debbie Dillman's mother."

"Huh?" said Brandon. Debbie Dillman had been one of Brenda's friends in Minneapolis.

"Don't you remember? When we were kids, I was in the backseat when she rammed that tree! That's why I'm great at everything except driving!"

Suddenly Brandon was very tired. His problem with James Townsend—his problem with himself—occupied his mind. He didn't care to joust with Brenda all night. "Sure, Brenda," he said. "You're a bad driver because somebody else ran into a tree eleven years ago. Good night."

With leaden feet, he walked to his bedroom, hoping that he would sleep through the night, and knowing that it was unlikely.

Early the next morning, Brandon sighed gratefully when the sky began to lighten. If he went to school now, he'd probably find the gym open. He'd have a chance to loosen up before anybody else got there. God knew he could use it. His muscles were as tight as piano wires.

When he got to school, Brandon not only found the gym open, he found a guy dribbling around and shooting baskets. It was James Townsend. Brandon stepped to the edge of the court and watched him for a while. When Townsend stopped and stood in the center of the court bouncing the ball, Brandon took a chance and called out, "You have a nice touch."

Surprised, Townsend looked in Brandon's direction, saw who it was, and between tight lips, said, "Thanks." He continued to bounce the ball.

Brandon said, "Listen. I thought a lot about what happened last night, and I can't pretend that in my mind, you were not guilty. But not because you were black; because with you out of the way, I'd have a better chance of making the team."

Townsend made a small nod and said, "It's true. Coach Reilly can pick only one of us." He stopped bouncing the ball and held it under one arm.

"The smart money's on you."

"Not necessarily. Not the way you play offense." Townsend shook his head and said, "Look, Brandon. You don't have to apologize for wanting this as bad as I do."

Townsend threw the ball, and it was only his trained reflexes that allowed Brandon to catch it. "You want to go one-on-one?" Townsend said.

Brandon smiled—with relief as much as with surprise for being asked. He and Townsend could now be friends. Maybe they wouldn't be bosom buddies, but you didn't ask an enemy to go one-on-one.

Brandon threw the ball back to Townsend and gave him the advantage of taking it out.

When the game was over—who won didn't matter—Brandon showered and went to find Andrea. He told her that there was no story in James Townsend after all. She was astounded, but seemed willing to let the matter rest, at least for the moment.

Townsend must have told his friends about the impromptu game with Brandon that morning, because when Brandon met Walker and DeWitt in the hall, instead of trying to scrag him, DeWitt called out, "Hey, Minnesota," and slipped him a high-five.

On his way home from school, Brandon stopped for a moment to enjoy the afternoon. High clouds, bright sunshine, a temp in the mid-seventies. If this was October, he'd take a dozen.

Evidently, Mrs. Walsh had also been influenced by the weather. She was at the top of the driveway poking at a barbecue fire with a long stick. "An outdoor barbecue in October," Brandon said. "I love it."

In the kitchen, Brenda was chopping onions. Brandon was eager to drop his stuff upstairs and come back down, but Brenda stopped him. "You'll be glad to hear," she said, "that Mr. Karton, the driver's training teacher, has agreed to sort of tutor me after school. He says that I might be a good driver someday, if I can control my death wish." She smiled ruefully.

"That's great, Bren. But it won't bring back Mondale."

"I'm working on it already," Brenda said. "Really."

Brandon gave her a look that said he'd believe it when he saw it. By the time he got back downstairs, his dad was home, also delighted and charmed by the idea of an outdoor barbecue in October. "So?" Mr. Walsh asked.

Brandon could not pretend to be ignorant of what his dad was talking about. He shrugged and said, "It got down to me and this other guy. Anyway, the coach thinks I could use a year on the B team under my belt."

Dad nodded. "Makes sense."

Dad was putting up a good front, but Brandon knew how much his getting the first string meant. He said, "Sorry, Dad."

"Sorry about what? About getting in some quality playing instead of riding the bench?"

"Not the same as nailing a shot at the buzzer with the whole school watching."

Mr. Walsh pursed his lips and then seemed to make a decision. He said, "Brandon, I have to tell you. That shot was just a fluke. The only reason I was playing at all was because everybody else had fouled out. It was either put in Walsh or forfeit the game."

His dad sounded really bummed. Brandon tried to lighten things up by saying, "Still, that was a pretty decent shot for a dinosaur."

"This dinosaur is going to kick your butt in horse. Uh, two out of three."

He and Brandon smiled. Brandon was about to get the ball when a police tow truck rolled up their driveway, honking like mad. Hanging precariously from the winch was Mondale!

"I never thought I'd see that puppy again," Brandon cried.

"Neither did I," Brenda said with some relief.

As Detective Kenner passed around papers for Mr. Walsh and Brandon to sign, he said, "It was the screwiest thing. Evidently, the perps weren't exactly rocket scientists. They left the car in the middle of an intersection. One of our trucks found it and towed it to the impound lot last night."

Clearing the emotional decks, Mrs. Walsh said, "The important thing is that it's back, and in one piece, and everything's great."

Detective Kenner said, "The amazing thing is that they left the keys in the ignition." From his pocket he pulled out Brandon's keys on a key chain featuring a puffy pink pom-pom. Brenda's eyes went wide.

"Isn't that your key chain?" Mrs. Walsh said.

Mr. and Mrs. Walsh tactfully waited until Detective Kenner was gone, and then they interrogated Brenda good. She ended up admitting what she had done.

Brandon could tell that their parents weren't pleased, but the fact that they could not quite keep from smiling at Brenda's bad luck meant that their judgment would not be too terrible. The fact that Mondale had actually been returned, and that Mr. Karton was going to tutor Brenda, softened them up even more. She got off with a stiff warning.

After the barbecue, which was an enormous success, everyone went into the house to digest. Homework was done. TV was watched. Books were read. Around eleven, Brandon was ready to hit the sack, but something about the barbecue began to bother him. And then he knew what it was and he visited Brenda with his revelation. Brenda brushed her hair as she listened to him rant.

"Here it is, October, and we're having a heat wave. And the leaves—they're not turning any color but brown. And the Air Quality Index! The very fact that one exists means our lungs are rotting with every breath we take."

"And earthquakes," Brenda said. "The last time you got like this, you talked about earthquakes."

"Them too."

"Do you really think—"

"I don't know. It's like the air, like this big looming thing that could change your life at any moment."

Downstairs, the phone rang and Brenda said, "I hope it's not for me. Dad hates it when my friends call after eleven, so he tells them I'm asleep. It's so embarrassing."

Brenda was safe. Mr. Walsh came to the door with an unreadable smile on his face. He said, "It's for you, Brandon."

"That's unusual," Brandon said and glanced at

Brenda to see what effect his statement had made. Brenda was pretending not to have heard. "Who is it?" Brandon asked.

"It's Sheryl."

That was a shock to Brandon, but it was a pleasant shock. His body turned hot and then cold and he smiled like a goof as he ran downstairs to get the phone.

21

True romance

MATHEMATICS, AS SUCH, WAS NOT BRENDA'S favorite class. That was to say, the academic part of math was not her favorite. But the teacher! What a hunk that Mr. Brody was: the best parts of Christopher Reeve, Sean Connery, and Mel Gibson all in one gorgeous package.

When he asked Brenda to stay after class for no reason at all, her heart, as the romance novels said, skipped a beat. She could almost see him leaning close, almost feel his hot masculine breath, almost hear him saying, *"Run away with me, Brenda. Let's make a love nest in some small alpine village where nobody knows our names. During the day, I'll teach skiing. At night, we'll cuddle by the fire, drink hot cider, and think how lucky we were to escape this tawdry Beverly Hills existence."*

As profound as her crush was, Brenda knew a fantasy when she saw one. Time for a reality check. She said, "Excuse me?"

Mr. Brody was still standing at the board. He said, "I asked if you could baby-sit for me and my wife on Saturday night."

Reality could be so disappointing. "Sure," she answered half-heartedly. Mr. Brody wrote down his address and asked her to be there at eight.

Brenda sighed. She'd take what she could get. What she got, mostly, was a lot of ribbing from Kelly and Donna about her and Mr. Brody. Kelly and Donna could be such children.

Brandon found Andrea at her locker and asked to be relieved from covering the big game with Beverly on Saturday night. He was so secretive and oblique that at first Andrea couldn't figure out why he wanted out. Then she smiled and said, "Who is she?"

"What are you, psychic?"

"No. I just recognize the signs."

Brandon looked down the hall but did not actually see it. He saw only Sheryl as he remembered her, cute, smiling, long blond hair—though she did not normally wear the kind of leather jumpsuit in which Brandon imagined her. Dreamily, he said, "My old girlfriend from Minneapolis. She's coming to visit for the weekend."

Softer, trying to be just a pal, Andrea asked, "How long were you guys together?"

"A year. Then Dad was transferred and we cut each other loose. I don't believe in long-distance relationships."

"A whole year. Wow. I never knew you had a girl-friend, Brandon."

Brandon shrugged. He was suddenly aware that every one of Andrea's questions had at least two meanings. He said, "It just seems stupid to talk about someone who's never around."

They both thought about that. Andrea said she would find somebody else to cover the game, then walked off, busy as Alice's White Rabbit.

Brandon didn't notice, but for the rest of the day he was either a major pain or he was mentally not there at all. He stared into space a lot, and when he finally spoke, it was generally about how beautiful Sheryl was, or about the outstanding quality of her personality, or about her funny little laugh. Dylan obviously had a low tolerance for this sort of mooning because in tech class, he said, "Give me a break, Brandon. She sleeps with you, so of course you think she's special."

"I didn't say that."

Dylan's eyebrows went up. Wonderingly, he said, "You mean she *doesn't* sleep with you?"

Actually, they never had. By the time Brandon felt right about asking, he and his family were on their way to California. He said, "I didn't say that either." Trying to be very cool, aloof, and mysterious, Brandon assumed an attitude of sophisticated boredom and walked away.

By the end of the day, Brandon had worked himself into a lovesick frenzy. Brenda had white knuckles as she gripped Mondale's dashboard. "Must you drive like a maniac?" she asked. "Her plane doesn't land for three hours."

Brandon slowed down and breathed deeply, as if he were at the freethrow line about to take a shot. He then made the mistake of asking Brenda if she thought he'd changed since coming to Beverly Hills.

"Oh, yes. In fact, she probably won't recognize you."

Hoping he looked like Clint Eastwood, Brandon gave Brenda an angry glance.

"A joke, Brandon, okay? Sheesh! Lighten up."

Lighten up. Sure. He still had time to get flowers. And some candy. And maybe one of those stuffed dogs she liked. His plans collapsed when he turned into the driveway and saw Sheryl standing outside the front door with his mom. He almost ran into the side of the house.

Mrs. Walsh chirped on about how Sheryl had taken an earlier flight, and since her arrival had been reporting the lowdown on all the lastest Minneapolis news. Sheryl just stared at Brandon, smiling. Brandon enjoyed returning the smile while he waited with growing nervousness for his mom to leave them alone. When she was in enthusiastic-extrovert mode, she could chirp on for hours.

"See you guys later, right, Mom?" Brenda said. "Right, Mom?"

Mrs. Walsh noticed what she was doing, welcomed Sheryl again, and went into the house with Brenda.

"Hi," Brandon said after a while.

"Hi."

They went up to Brandon's room and sat on the bed leafing through the high-school yearbook from the previous year. Brandon was amazed and gratified that Sheryl had memorized all the pages where the two of them appeared together.

They moved closer together on the bed, and somehow they were hugging and then they were kissing and Brandon felt himself losing control, just feeling Sheryl's body against his.

A knock at the door came like a pistol shot and

they leaped apart. The yearbook fell to the floor. Brandon dived for it and Sheryl said, "We were just looking at last year's yearbook."

Mrs. Walsh stood in the doorway with an armload of bed linen and towels. She sounded a little embarrassed when she said, "Sheryl, I just wanted to show you where you'd be sleeping."

Mom's timing was impeccable. Brandon wondered what would have happened if she hadn't arrived just then. He smiled, thinking it would have been fun to find out. Kidding her, he said, "I can show Sheryl where Brenda's room is."

Mrs. Walsh jacked up a smile and said, "Just trying to be helpful. Brandon, can I get you to help me with something in the kitchen?"

"Sure, Mom. Be right down."

When Mrs. Walsh was gone, Brandon and Sheryl laughed. He said, "Mom's pretty subtle."

"Plenty of time," Sheryl said. "I'll be here all weekend."

Dinner was fun. Sheryl and Mom monopolized the conversation, talking about people in Minneapolis that Brandon had barely known. Nobody seemed to mind. Brandon certainly didn't. He just liked listening to the sound of Sheryl's voice.

Later, while Brandon got ready for bed, he heard Brenda and Sheryl discussing teachers and old boyfriends and giggling. Brandon pulled back the covers on his bed and ran his hand across the cool clean sheets. Very nice. He pushed into the mattress a couple of times and critically listened to the telltale squeak. Not too bad. He checked to make certain the foil packet was in the drawer of his night table. It was. He was as ready as he would ever be.

22

Tests of manhood

WATER RAN IN THE BATHROOM.

Brenda was singing in her room, so the person running the water had to be Sheryl. Brandon slipped on a pair of gym shorts and knocked.

"Come in," Sheryl said.

Brandon opened the door and saw that Sheryl looked only terrific in her Mickey Mouse nightshirt. He took her into his arms and whispered into her ear, "Come to my room in an hour." Gosh, she felt good. She smelled good, too.

Brandon heard an intake of breath, and then Sheryl asked, "What if your parents check on us? What if they hear?"

"They won't." He kissed the tip of her nose. "I promise." He kissed her right cheek. "They sleep like the dead." He kissed her left cheek. "Don't say no." He kissed her chin.

"I don't know," Sheryl said, and looked toward Brenda's room.

Brandon tried to hang on to his cool. He could see that it was time to be masterful. He put his hand on her arm and said firmly, "Forty-five minutes."

"I have to think about it." She flashed him a nervous smile and slipped back into Brenda's room.

This situation was maddening. Did this girl live in the fifties or what? Was she some kind of Victorian? He was in his sexual prime. Use it or lose it. Brandon lay down on his bed and tried to be calm. He waited. Time passed. The giggling from Brenda's room became less frequent and then stopped altogether. His parents' bed creaked. Cars went by. Dogs barked far away.

Brandon had given up and was, almost against his will, falling asleep, when his door opened slowly and a shape crossed the room. He smiled. Sheryl slid into the bed next to him and they nuzzled.

"Hi," Brandon said.

"Hi."

They enfolded each other and rolled across the bed. It squeaked and they froze for a moment. Nothing. Just night-time sounds. His parents slept like dead things. Brandon relaxed and felt Sheryl relax on top of him. He whispered, "If we had to move two thousand miles so you could come spend the night, I think it was worth the trouble."

Sheryl pulled back and looked at him seriously. She said, "Do you have protection? I mean—"

He put his finger to her lips and said, "Of course. Lots of protection. But up till now, no one to protect."

"Let's see if we can change that." She put her hands on Brandon's chest and then worked her way lower.

■ ■ ■

The next day dawned warm and bright. If it had been cold and dingy, Brandon would have loved it just the same. He put on a compact disk of big-band hits from the forties and programmed the player to play "In the Mood" over and over again.

Swinging to the music, he got dressed, then went downstairs. In a fit of uncharacteristic morning energy, he squeezed oranges for juice. Sheryl came downstairs in jeans and a conservative—read: purchased in Minnesota—halter top. Still glowing from the previous night, they kissed. Brenda caught them, but she seemed singularly casual about the entire thing. "Don't mind me," she said. She saw the orange juice Brandon had made and confided to Sheryl, "Trust me. He never does this. *Never.*"

Sheryl wanted to see movie stars, most specifically, Tom Cruise. Brandon tried not to make rash promises, but he thought it might be a good idea to escape before his parents came down. Just in case, while thrashing around like wounded alligators, they'd made more noise than they'd supposed.

"I don't believe this, Brandon," Brenda called to them as they ran out the door. "You even strained the pulp!"

For the next few hours, Brandon showed Sheryl the Beverly Hills and Hollywood the tourists always see. They saw big houses that may once have been inhabited by movie stars. They saw cars too exotic to be identified. They saw fancy women and handsome men. They tried on footprints for size at the Chinese Theater. Tom Cruise seemed to be in hiding.

While Brandon drove them across town to the Bel

Age for lunch—just the coffee shop, not the dining room—Sheryl said, "This place is amazing. I want to move here."

Despite Sheryl's presence, Brandon had found the last few hours increasingly wearing. His interest in seeing movie stars was minimal, and he knew from sad experience that the chances of recognizing one of them on the street was even less. Without the lights and the makeup and the costumes, they just looked like ordinary people. Besides, he'd actually lived in Los Angeles for several months, and he knew it had its soft seamy underbelly just like anyplace else. He said, "You don't really want to live here. You'd be homesick in a minute."

With all the assurance of a novice, Sheryl said, "I think you've got a warped view of Minneapolis, Brandon."

"Could be," Brandon said. Better not to argue. Better to enjoy the day, the moment, the woman.

At the Bel Age Hotel, Brandon decided to splurge and use the valet parking. Inside, the hotel was still the same grand Pharaoh's tomb of a place. But the Bel Age coffee shop was just like any other coffee shop except the fittings were brass instead of chrome, more potted plants stood around, and each dish cost about twice what it would elsewhere.

Sheryl rubbernecked the room, saw no one interesting, and accused Brandon of taking her there only because he was hungry.

"Even movie stars eat," he said. "And there's somebody I want you to meet."

A waitress came over with menus. She was not one of the beautiful people. She wore practical shoes, and was a little hunchy, and her lined face contained eyes that would not betray surprise. "Are any stars here today?" Sheryl asked hopefully.

The waitress gave her the fish eye and without interest said, "You'll be the first to know, honey." She walked away.

Brandon took Sheryl's hands across the table and smiled at her. She smiled back. Brandon said, "Well, we finally got it right." Oblivious of the other diners, they leaned around the table and kissed.

A loud voice behind them said, "I thought I asked for the no-smooching section."

It was Dylan, of course. As proud as if he'd invented both of them, Brandon introduced Dylan and Sheryl. Dylan sat down and said, "Brandon speaks so highly of you, I thought he was making you up."

Sheryl blushed and said, "Shucks."

Brandon said, "Dylan lives at this hotel."

While Sheryl marveled at that, Brandon stood up and said, "Excuse me. I have to use the bathroom. Another thing movie stars sometimes do." He kissed Sheryl on the forehead and walked off.

The bathroom was really something, too. It did the basic job, but in surroundings even the more decadent Caesars might have found to be ostentatious.

When he came back, Brandon asked, "See anybody worth mentioning?"

A little embarrassed, Sheryl said, "No. But Dylan knows this great club where we might see movie stars."

"Yeah?" Brandon said as he sat down. For Sheryl's benefit, he turned up the gain on his interest.

"It's called Contact," Dylan said. "Very private. But I can get you guys in. If you have no other plans for tonight."

This was obviously a done deal, but before Brandon had a chance to buy into it, their waitress came back, order book in hand, and said, "Nobody yet, honey." Even Sheryl had to laugh.

Sheryl and Brenda stood in front of the mirror in Brenda's room gauging the effectiveness of their respective outfits. Sheryl wore a very nice skirt and black pumps and had sufficiently frizzed her hair. Brenda was aware of where she was going, and why, so she was even more conservatively dressed, but tried to make up for it with accessories. "What do you think of these earrings?" she asked, and touched one of them with a finger. The big tin spirals dangled nearly to her shoulders.

"Boss. Or whatever you say here. They're cute."

"Not too queer or dangly?"

"What's the big deal, Brenda? You're only baby-sitting."

"I'm baby-sitting for Mr. Brody. That gorgeous teacher I told you about? Matt?"

"Oh, my God," Sheryl said, suddenly aware of the critical nature of the situation. "You're going to be in his house? You're going to meet his wife?"

Brenda nodded.

"Let's take another look," Sheryl said.

Brandon looked at himself in the mirror by the front door and shot his cuffs. He was a symphony in black and white. For the thousandth time he checked his earlobes. Would earrings look good on him? He was repelled by the thought. Maybe he hadn't been in

Beverly Hills long enough. "Come on, ladies," he called up the stairs.

Mr. Walsh came into the foyer with a serious expression on his face. Not angry, just serious. Hoping he was wrong about what was coming, Brandon composed his face along similar lines.

"Brandon, we need to talk." Mr. Walsh put his arm around Brandon's shoulder and guided him to the couch in the living room.

"What's the problem, Dad?"

"No problem." Mr. Walsh seemed pensive for a moment. Then he said, "You like Sheryl a lot, don't you?"

Bingo, thought Brandon. Still, there was no point rushing things. Let Dad make his play. "Yeah, Dad. I do."

"And you would never do anything to hurt her, would you?"

"Of course not."

"Of course not." Mr. Walsh thought more before he said, "You know, Brandon, you're not a kid anymore. In many ways, you're an adult."

"You mean like sexually, Dad?"

"Uh, yes. And that means that sexually, you need to be as responsible as an adult would be. *More* responsible than some adults."

Brandon nodded.

Outside, a horn honked. "Excuse me, Dad." Brandon ran for the door, swung it open, and called to Dylan that they would be right out. Brenda and Sheryl leaped down the stairs and clumped at the door with Brandon.

Mr. Walsh came to the door. Brandon said, "Anything else, Dad?" He guessed that Dad had not yet covered the part about Brandon pretending Sheryl was his sister.

Mr. Walsh looked uncomfortably at Brenda and

Sheryl and said, "Uh, no. Have a good time."

"Bye-yee, Dad," Brenda said, and left.

"Bye-yee, Mr. Walsh," Sheryl said, and left.

Brandon was bemused. He shrugged and bowed to fashion. "Bye-yee, Dad." He walked outside and down to the street where the two girls stood admiring Dylan's Porsche.

"Can I sit in it?" Sheryl asked. Her eyes were big as saucers. Obviously, she had never seen a car as cool as Dylan's. Brandon felt a little embarrassed on Mondale's behalf.

"Come on, Sheryl," said Brandon. "We have to drop off Brenda at the baby-sit."

Sheryl laid her hand on Brandon's chest and asked quietly if she could ride with Dylan.

Brandon understood that a Porsche was not just any car. He understood that Dylan was one of his best friends, maybe his very best friend. But Sheryl's request worried him. He was tempted to say no, just to see if she would go anyway. Come on, Brandon. This wasn't a test of manhood. It was just a ride in a car. "Sure," he said. "If that's what you want."

Brandon watched silently as Sheryl climbed into the Porsche next to Dylan. Brenda started yelling about how late she was, and then the Porsche was gone, and then Brandon had no further excuse to stand there on the front lawn like a dope.

23

The personal touch

MR. BRODY LIVED IN AN UNDISTINGUISHED Spanish-style house on a street lined with undistinguished Spanish-style houses. Brandon dropped Brenda out front, and barely waited for her to get to the house before he gunned Mondale's engine and was gone.

Mr. Brody answered the door wearing a very nice sport coat and pants in two gentle shades of brown. He smiled that dynamic smile and asked her to come in. "Nice earrings," he said as she passed him in the doorway.

It was an older house, with earthquake cracks in the chalky white paint on the walls and ceiling. The slightly stale smell of the house reminded Brenda of her grandparents. None of the furniture matched. Toys were everywhere. It was a pleasant jumble, but not quite what Brenda had pictured for the dashing Mr. Brody.

And Brenda was not sure that Mrs. Brody was

good enough for him. She was a thin, nervous blonde who was pretty enough in an anorexic way, but had all the warmth of a tile bathroom. She introduced the children, Lisa and Elliot.

Lisa was about eight, and felt she was old enough to stay home without a baby-sitter. Elliot was four. He held on to his mother's leg and seemed unwilling to let go. Brenda smiled hopefully. They eyed her suspiciously, as if she had already done them dirt.

Mrs. Brody's smile at Brenda came and went with the speed of lightning. She looked at her husband disapprovingly and said, "Call Dan and tell them we're running late. And not that jacket."

Mr. Brody looked down at himself and said, "Why not?"

"Because you're wearing two shades of the same color, that's why not. And hurry, or we'll never make the movie." Mrs. Brody marched off toward what Brenda assumed was the kitchen.

When Mr. Brody climbed the stairs, he looked back at Brenda and smiled wanly. Brenda smiled with encouragement. She felt awful. The kids were awful. Mrs. Brody was the worst. How could Mr. Brody exist in such absolute squalor? Could she exist in it for a whole evening?

Brandon found Contact at last. He circled the block a few times and spotted what looked like Dylan's Porsche, and then had to circle again before he found a parking space of his own.

He walked around to the front of the big white building and scoped the line behind the red velvet rope. He saw the usual assortment of urban cowboys, pseudo-sophisticates, studied ragamuffins, and aging hippies. Many of them were holding up the building. They had been there a long time. Only the fact that even standing in line here made one more hip gave them the strength to stay. It's tough being hip when your name isn't on the list. Making sure that nobody got in who wasn't supposed to was a tuxedoed bouncer the size of Cleveland. The city, not the president. Maybe he was a sumo wrestler.

The important thing was that Dylan and Sheryl weren't out there waiting for him. Brandon would have to go inside to look for them. But before he could find out if *his* name was on the list, a girl wearing green sparkles and a skirt seemingly made from a facecloth rushed the bouncer with two of her equally in-your-face companions. That distracted the bouncer long enough for Brandon to duck inside. Behind him he heard shouts of protest, but he kept moving.

He stopped just inside the door because he was astonished by what he saw. The floor, walls, and ceiling were painted a flat black. Things stuck out from every surface—mostly neon or chrome things. The theme for the evening was *contact*: electrical contact, person-to-person contact, contact paper, contact! (as in starting your airplane), contacts (as in knowing the right people)—Brandon probably missed some of the more obscure puns. The bar looked as if it were made from the bodies of two pink Cadillacs that had contacted in a head-on collision. The crowd inside the building looked pretty much like the crowd outside.

Brandon spotted Sheryl and Dylan dancing with a lot of other couples under some kind of alien mother ship flashing in time to the music. She leaned in close to hear something Dylan said and then threw back her head and laughed.

Brandon was relieved to find them, but he hadn't imagined them dancing together. He definitely hadn't imagined that Sheryl would enjoy Dylan's jokes quite so much. He definitely hadn't imagined that he could get so angry so suddenly.

He wove his way through the dancers. Dylan saw him and waved. He shouted against the music, "Hey, Minnesota! Over here!" A person who did not shout at Contact was not heard.

"I see that you guys are getting acquainted," Brandon said, an edge in his voice.

"Dylan's a wonderful dancer," Sheryl said.

"Yeah, well, let me know when the lesson is over. I'll be at the bar."

Sheryl seemed surprised and then angered by Brandon's tone. She said, "Fine, Brandon. You can dance with him now. I'm going to the bathroom." She walked straight off the dance floor, miraculously without bumping into anyone.

Brandon was aware that he and Dylan were standing in the middle of a crowded dance floor, two stags with their hands in their pockets. They looked pretty silly, if anybody noticed. But Brandon was so steamed, he wanted to have it out with Dylan right then and there.

Dylan tried to smooth things over by shouting appreciatively, "She is *wild*, Brandon."

But Brandon was beyond smooth talk. "Dylan, you can probably go out with any girl in the whole damned school. Why hit on my girlfriend?"

Dylan shook his head, astonished. "You're out of your mind, man. I didn't hit on her."

"Of course not. But it was, 'Hey, I know this cool club I can get us into,' and it was, 'Check out my car,' and it was, 'Let's just go in—Brandon will find us,' and

'Let me buy you a drink,' and 'Wow, that's my favorite song, too,' and—

"And that's not how it happened, Brandon." Even shouting, Dylan sounded cold and deadly. But Brandon just didn't care. He thought he'd been hurt, and the truth of the matter would have to wait for another time.

"It doesn't work with Sheryl, Dylan. She's only into one guy."

Dylan shook his head. "If that's what you think, you two should have a serious talk. Because Brandon, as much as I hate to tell you this, your girlfriend hit on *me* tonight."

For a moment, they were eye to eye. Brandon couldn't believe what he was hearing. Dylan obviously saw himself as some kind of Don Juan and had imagined everything. He was knocking Sheryl's reputation. He was. . . Brandon briefly lost the ability to be verbal. He growled and leaped at Dylan, knocking him to the floor. Brandon stood over him, waiting for the inevitable fight.

Though he was surprised, if not actually dazed, Dylan got to his feet and grabbed Brandon's shirtfront in both hands. "Figure out who your friends are, nimrod," Dylan said, and pushed Brandon hard. Brandon hit the floor and slid a few feet. He watched Dylan walk among the dancing couples and into the darkness. Had Brandon solved his problem, or had he just screwed up everything royally?

Brenda never wanted to have children, not ever. After tonight she never wanted to see children again. Not even the pleasure of doing something for Mr. Brody could lure her back to this house.

Being a girl, Lisa had potential, but at her age she grew bored easily. Games had been pulled out of closets with excitement and delight only to be abandoned ten minutes later. And now they were running out of games.

Elliot was going through something Brenda's mother would probably call *a stage*. In the absence of his mother, he had clamped himself to Brenda's leg. Also, he would invite Brenda to ask questions to which only he knew the answers. One time Elliot informed her that he would be five on his next birthday and that he wanted a red bicycle. Another time, Elliot informed her that his father (Mr. Brody!) had a penis.

"And you know what?" Elliot said.

"No," said Brenda in exasperation. "And I don't want to know."

The doorbell rang, preventing Elliot from inviting Brenda to once again "Guess what." Visions of ax murderers danced in her head while Brenda limped to the door with Elliot attached to one leg. Trying to sound brave, she called through the door, "Who is it?"

"It's us," two teenage-girl voices said together.

Brenda knew she should never have told them where she would be. Giving them a hard time, Brenda said, "Us who?"

"The Big Bad Wolf," Kelly said.

"And her friend the Terminator," Donna said.

Hardy-har-har. Brenda put out her hand to open the door. Lisa called out from the living room, where she was forcing her game piece to walk up a ladder on the Chutes and Ladders board. "Mom says never to open the door for strangers."

Definitely strange, thought Brenda, but not strangers. "Thank you, Lisa," Brenda said, and opened the door.

Kelly and Donna entered, gawking as if Mr. Brody's dorky house were some kind of cathedral. "We wanted to see where he lived," Kelly said.

Somebody around here had to be responsible.

Brenda said, "This is exactly the kind of thing Mr. Brody didn't want."

"Guess what?" Elliot asked.

"What?" said Donna.

Was Elliot going to talk about Mr. Brody's anatomy again? Brenda held her breath.

Elliot said, "I have toys in my room. I'll show you." He took one of Donna's hands.

Lisa grabbed the other and said, "I have makeup," as if she were one of the favored few.

Kelly looked down at Elliot and said, "When you grow up, I bet you'll be a hunk, just like your dad."

Evidently Elliot liked what he heard because he let go of Donna's hand and attached himself to Kelly's leg. She looked uncomfortable.

Brenda smiled with satisfaction. They had asked for it.

In the next half hour, Brandon found out what an impersonal place Contact could be if you were there alone—and he felt that no one was more alone than he. Contact was a big dark place, full of bodies, loud sounds and the smells of alcohol, fancy perfume, and manly aftershave. What it seemed to have a shortage of was Sheryl.

He worked his way through yet another crowd, excusing himself as he went. On the other side of it, he saw Sheryl. She was sitting at the smashed Cadillac bar with a tall cool one in her hand. Brandon didn't think the glass held soda pop.

He blindsided her, grabbed her arm and said, "Come on. We're out of here."

Sheryl stared at him without interest for a moment and then recognized him. She seemed to speak from the far side of an alcoholic haze when she asked, "Where's Dylan?"

No question could have made Brandon angrier. He said, "What possible difference could that make?"

Sheryl pulled her arm away and downed another big swallow. Brandon was sure she was wasted. He almost wished that he was, too. Ignoring Brandon's general rage, Sheryl looked around and said, "This place is so cool. Once you're in, they don't even card you at the bar. Minneapolis has nothing like this."

Brandon decided to try another approach. He didn't like being angry, anyway. With some tenderness, he pulled the drink from Sheryl's semirigid fingers and set it on the bar. "I think you've had one too many," he said as gently as possible against the music.

Sheryl gave him a poisonous glare and said, "Don't you *ever* tell me what to do."

This wasn't the kind, loving Sheryl he knew at all. Not even the alcohol could account for her behavior. He said, "What's going on, Sheryl? This isn't you." He looked at her with concern.

"How would *you* know, Brandon?" She picked up her glass and downed the remains of her drink in one long gulp. He was as horrified as if he'd discovered that Brenda was doing drugs. Sheryl's glass thumped when she set it down. "You haven't seen me in six months. *People change*."

Brandon ran a hand through his hair. Nothing made sense except the frustration he felt. "Jesus, after last night . . ." He shook his head. "I thought we'd be closer than ever."

"Grow up, Brandon. Sex doesn't make people closer. It just tears them apart."

Sex? What happened to *making love*? "What makes you such an expert?"

"Because I've done it before."

Brandon had not even seen the punch coming and he was not prepared for it. Sheryl's words struck him with almost physical force. He put his hand on the bar for balance and collapsed onto a stool. He was certain he looked drunker than Sheryl did.

Evidently, Sheryl had seen the impact her admission had made on Brandon because she shrugged and said, "What difference does it make? It just happened."

It just happened. Rage built again in Brandon. He'd never felt so jerked around in his life. He shouted, "A hell of a difference. After you made me wait, and wait, and wait! Who was it?" He grabbed her arm again, this time more roughly. He wanted his grip to hurt. "I want names *now*, or you can catch the next bus back to Minneapolis."

She pulled away from him and stood up, a little unsteadily. "Fine. You don't have to ask me twice." She slapped a few bills on the bar and staggered away.

Brandon wanted to follow her, explain things, apologize, anything to once again make Sheryl the sweet girl he'd known. Then he decided, why bother? Let Dylan handle it. Then he wanted to follow her again. On the one hand. On the other hand.

He didn't really make a decision, but his feet moved him in the direction of the door. Too late, evidently. He forced his way through the milling crowd outside and saw her getting into a cab. He raced for the cab, crying, "Sheryl, wait!" but the cab was already moving. Brandon sprinted after it. By the time he reached the corner and stopped, it was long gone.

His face throbbed with heat in time with the pounding of his heart. He was crying. He felt wretched. He didn't know what to do.

A car honked at him and he got out of the street.

24

A time for ice cream

BRANDON SHOOK HIS HEAD AT HIS OWN FOOL-
ishness. Getting out of the street had been a good start
on repairing the evening, but he went to sit in Mondale
so he could think without a crowd around. Dylan.
Dylan was the key to this whole thing. Sheryl knew he
lived at the Bel Age. Brandon was certain that's where
she would go. Besides, Sheryl wasn't exactly the type
to leave town on a *bus*.

The Bel Age was a short drive away, and Brandon
didn't remember any of it. He left Mondale in the self-
park lot and went up to Dylan's suite. He knocked
calmly on the door, but when he didn't get an immedi-
ate answer, he knocked more loudly, and soon was
pounding with his fist.

Dylan answered the door, admitted Sheryl was
there, and invited Brandon to come in. Brandon

walked to the middle of the room, whirled on Dylan, and said, "Where is she?"

Dylan clicked the door shut and looked at Brandon for a moment before he said, "At the moment, Brandon, she's in my bathroom being sick." He shook his head. "But listen: I never made a move on her, I swear. And she's not into me. That's not what this is all about."

Dylan sounded so calm, so reasonable, he pulled Brandon along with him. Brandon took a couple of deep breaths. Trying to match Dylan's cool, he said, "Then what is it all about? Right now I'm a man without a clue."

"Ask Sheryl. The girl has some problems."

"Yeah. Why does Beverly Hills have this effect on people?"

"Hey, don't put this off onto Beverly Hills. She has *Minneapolis* problems."

A toilet flushed, and a few seconds later Sheryl entered the room slowly, looking pale and fragile. She seemed surprised to see Brandon, but she was no longer angry. She was just a little girl far away from home. "Hi," she said.

She looked so lost and lonely that Brandon almost forgave her everything. But she had done some things he could not yet forgive. "Hi," he said, not giving her an inch.

While Dylan rubbed his hands together and backed toward the door he said, "I'm just going to kind of slip away right now. If you guys want anything— room service, clean towels—don't hesitate to call downstairs."

When the door closed behind Dylan, Sheryl picked up a water glass from an end table and sipped carefully. This gave Brandon the chance to say, "So. Are you going to tell me what's going on? The drinking? The carrying on? The running out of that club?"

Sheryl put down the glass and said, "You don't know me at all, Brandon." Her voice was hard.

Brandon realized he was threatening her by standing in the middle of the room. The time for threatening was over. He sat on the couch opposite her. "What are you talking about?"

"Those last few weeks in Minneapolis, all you talked about was how tough things were going to be for you. But you came to paradise and made a new life with new friends while I stayed where the only reason people wear sunglasses in October is so they don't go snowblind."

"I didn't think things were so bad with you."

Suddenly stronger, Sheryl said, "How would you know? I never talked about the stepfather that I hate and the mother who defends him. I didn't tell you about the father that never calls, not even on my birthday."

"You hid it pretty well."

"It was easy because you were rarely at my house. I was always at yours. But that's okay, because when we were together, or with your family, I felt safe. I didn't have to think about things." She looked at him accusingly. "But when you moved, Brandon, it was like everything closed in on me." She began to cry.

Brandon couldn't stand it anymore. He moved to sit next to her and tentatively put his arm around her. She leaned into him and sobbed. Through her tears, she said, "I thought if I came here, things would be better. But seeing you again only made everything worse."

Great, thought Brandon. The Minnesota Monster. He patted her shoulder and said, "Do you want to go home?"

Sheryl straightened up and wiped her eyes. "I guess I should at least call my mom. Let her know where I am."

"Let her what?"

Sheryl giggled and sniffled at the same time, which was kind of endearing, but Brandon was too shocked to appreciate it.

"Oh yes. There's one more thing I forgot to mention. I didn't come here just to see you, Brandon. I ran away from home."

Brandon could see they had a lot of talking ahead of them. In his family, when it was time for serious discussions, only one thing would do. He went to the phone and could already hear the dial tone when Sheryl asked worriedly, "Who are you calling?"

"Room service. We need ice cream, Sheryl. Lots of ice cream. It's the only way to deal with this."

Getting Lisa and Elliot into bed was a major operation. And once they were there, they needed a bedtime story and glasses of water and good-night kisses. Brenda thought about what her friends put substitute teachers through, and wondered how much of what Lisa and Elliot claimed to be normal really was.

Brenda came limply downstairs wondering how *her* parents had lived through *her* childhood. Maybe it was easier when you got older. From the living room came giggling and Arsenio Hall.

"Look at this," said Kelly.

"God," said Donna. "Matt was such a major babe."

Brenda found her friends sitting hip to hip on the couch before a coffee table littered with soda cans, bags of chips, and cookie crumbs. They were flipping through a photograph album. Brenda looked on the rowdy scene with despair.

Kelly had found the album in Mr. Brody's underwear drawer, of all places. Brenda absolutely did not want to know why Kelly was poking around there in the first place, but she could not help glancing at the photos.

"I think he got married way too young," Donna said.

A key jiggled at the front door. Brenda and her friends froze. Then Brenda leaped to her feet as Mr. and Mrs. Brody entered. Before she even said hello, Mrs. Brody shrieked, "Matt, what are they doing with our wedding album?"

Behind his wife, Mr. Brody made an *oops!* face and said, "I'm sure it was just lying around."

Mrs. Brody surveyed the junk-food carnage and began to snatch up cans and plastic bags.

"I didn't think you'd be home this early," Brenda said as she helped Mrs. Brody gather the trash.

"Obviously," said Mrs. Brody, putting a nasty spin on it. "Such a pleasure, Matt, to see a bad movie and then come home to this."

"Yes. Well. How much do we owe you, Brenda?"

Brenda hoped her smile looked more natural than it felt. "Whatever you think is right." Just let me out of here in once piece, and I'll be fine, Brenda thought.

They escaped poor Mr. Brody and his witch-queen wife and Kelly drove Brenda home. Kelly and Donna spoke of nothing but what a babe Mr. Brody was and how he had a crush on Brenda. Brenda did not take part. She was thinking.

Finally, she said, "You know how you can be totally into some gorgeous guy, on TV or something, and then you see in a magazine what he really looks like and read what he really thinks and you wonder, where was my mind?"

Kelly and Donna waited for the hammer to come down.

"That's what happened tonight with me and Mr. Brody."

"Brenda is so mature," Kelly said. She and Donna laughed.

I'm not suffering from maturity, Brenda thought. Just a healthy dose of reality. She thanked Kelly for the ride and then ran into the house, where she found her parents meditatively eating ice cream.

"What's wrong?" Brenda asked. She knew what eating ice cream in the middle of the night meant.

They told her that Sheryl's mother had called, worried sick. Sheryl wasn't just visiting. She'd run away after a fight with her stepfather.

Brenda grabbed a spoon and dipped into the open container.

As Brandon pulled into the driveway he saw that lights were on in the kitchen.

"Waiting up for us?" Sheryl asked.

"Maybe. But that's not like them."

Brandon and Sheryl came in through the backdoor. Mom, Dad, and Brenda looked up from bowls of ice cream and gaped at them as if they were ghosts. After a moment of tension, Mom said, "Sheryl, your mother called."

Sheryl wasn't even surprised. She just nodded and asked to use the phone. Mom offered her the one upstairs, where it would be private.

When Sheryl was gone, Dad said, "Brandon, grab some ice cream and join me in the living room. There's something I want to talk to you about."

He was pretty sure Dad would try to finish his sexual-responsibility speech, and Brandon wasn't up for it. He said, "Can it wait till tomorrow, Dad? I've had all the ice cream I want for one night."

"Maybe we all have. Tomorrow."

In his room, Brandon paged through the high-school yearbook trying to recapture the strong feelings he'd had about Sheryl before she arrived. After a while, he knew it was hopeless. He sat with the closed book in his lap. Brenda came in and sat down next to him on the bed.

Brandon said, "I thought I knew her, Bren."

"You can't see what people don't let you see."

"Yeah. But I thought we were close. She knew *everything* about me."

Brenda pushed him in the ribs. "Did she know how you used to eat Mom's makeup?"

Brandon could not help smiling. "I guess we weren't as close as I thought," he said.

Brenda stood and, from the doorway, said, "It's never too late."

"The only thing I want to say to Sheryl right now is good-bye."

"Hey, it's a start."

Despite his troubles, Brandon slept well that night. Nothing had been resolved, of course, but he felt that he had a handle on the situation. He could deal with it.

The next morning, he went to Brenda's room to see if Sheryl would let him drive her to the airport. She told him she had made other arrangements. Brandon looked for something else to say, something else to ask. "So. Are you and your parents going to work things out?"

"No choice. Real estate in LA is a little steep for me right now." She smiled the old smile. "But give me a few years. I'll be back." She picked up her suitcase and said, "I'm sorry, Brandon."

"Yeah. Me too."

Sheryl put down her suitcase and touched Brandon's hand. "But I want you to know about the other night when we made love. Brandon, we both know it wasn't my first time—for which you may never forgive me—but trust me, with you it was different."

His hand tingled where Sheryl touched it. "Different how?" he asked. They had more to talk about than he'd guessed.

Sheryl's eyes looked far away. Was she thinking about Brandon? About the other guys she'd known in the Biblical sense? Would he come up short—in any sense? She said, "It was like it's supposed to be. Like I imagined it would be. And it made me realize something." She leaned closer to him.

He leaned closer to her. Their lips almost touched. "What's that?" Brandon said.

Outside, a horn honked. Sheryl pulled away, ran to the window, and cried, "It's the shuttle. Got to go, Brandon." She pecked him on the cheek, said, "Write me a letter," and caught her suitcase as she ran.

"Sheryl, wait!"

He couldn't go through life or even the next minute like this. He had to know what Sheryl had realized. He ran from the room and, standing at the stop of the stairs, shouted, "Sheryl, what did you realize?"

Brenda came out of the kitchen with a sandwich in time to hear Sheryl shout back to him, "Brandon, you are an incredible lover!" Then she was out the door and gone.

Brenda giggled and backed into the kitchen. Brandon grinned. He felt pretty good. He wondered if anybody else had heard Sheryl, and couldn't decide how he felt about that, one way or the other. He heard somebody dribbling a basketball in the backyard. Dad. Brandon was in the mood for a game. Sure.

When he came out the backdoor, his dad was making incredible saves. "Hey, Dad," Brandon called. "Practicing behind my back, I see."

They just hacked around for a while, just shooting baskets and giving each other a hard time. Then Dad held the ball, bounced it a few times, and said, "You know, Brandon, when I was your age, my father told me that someday I would meet a girl who would break my heart. And then I'd meet one who wouldn't."

"Yeah?" This didn't sound like the responsibility lecture.

"The point is, Brandon, that Sheryl might be the right girl. She might not. Who knows? The point is, even the heartbreakers should be special. Get me?"

"Dad, are we talking about sex?"

"Actually, *I'm* talking about love." He pitched the ball and it went in. Neither of them went to get it. Dad said, "Why? Is there something you'd like to ask me about sex?"

"I don't know, Dad. Is anything new since we talked when I was ten?"

Dad looked bewildered. He shrugged and said, "I don't know. You tell me."

"Just tell Mom we were careful."

"She'll be glad to hear it."

Brandon got the ball. He and his dad played horse. Dad won two out of three and Brandon claimed it was because he felt sorry for such a geezer.

They played. They argued. They had a totally awesome time, just like they had in Minneapolis. After all, Minneapolis was just a location. It was people that counted.

Mel Gilden is the author of over 15 books for children and the bestselling novelization STAR TREK: THE NEXT GENERATION. He lives in California where he is currently at work on his next novelization for HarperPaperbacks.